Sabrina
The Teenage Witch™

C000227486

Contents

Sabrina The Teenage Witch™

Published by Pedigree Books Limited
Beech Hill House, Walnut Gardens, Exeter,
Devon EX4 4DG.
E-mail books@pedigreegroup.co.uk Published 2003

Pedigree®

Sabrina, the Teenage Witch ™ & © Archie Comic
Publications, Inc. © 2003 Viacom Productions Inc.
Based on characters in Archie Comics. All rights reserved.

visit
Sabrina
The Teenage
Witch
at
www.archiecomics.com

Meet the Gang!

Hi, everyone! And welcome to my third annual - and you know what witches say about the number three. It's always lucky! Now most of you know me, my family and friends already, but in case you've just come back from travelling through the fourth dimension with my dad (he's a warlock!), here's an update!

SABRINA SPELLMAN

First, there's me, Sabrina Spellman and I'm a witch! Don't worry, I don't go around flying on a vacuum (broomsticks are so 20th century). Well, not often! I'm just your every day teenager! (And, being a teenager is the best, if a bit confusing sometimes!)

I'm a Virgo (a good star sign for a witch!), and I'm currently studying journalism at Adams College in Boston. also work as an intern at the *Boston Citizen*, when I'm not working or hanging out at my Aunt Hilda's coffee shop.

My mom, Diana, is a mortal, and is on an archaeological dig in Peru – the reason being that the rotten Witches' Council doesn't take kindly to witches marrying mortals. So, once I turned 16 and got my powers, they said we could never see each other face-to-face again. (But we do, in this very annual! Ha!) I live in a house just off-campus with my roommates, who I'll tell you about in a minute…!

DIANA SPELLMAN

HILDA & ZELDA SPELLMAN

My wacky aunts, who raised me from my aforementioned 16th birthday when I found out I was a witch. They're just the best, and I love them loads! Aunt Zelda, (when not conducting bizarre experiments at their house!) teaches science at my college. She's been dating Professor Arthur Carlin from the university, but I've got a feeling it won't last! (None of her boyfriends ever do!) Aunt Hilda is a successful businesswoman (how, I don't know!) who owns the coffee house where I work. She's a little nutty – even by Spellman standards.

SALEM SABERHAGEN

Aww looks so cute, doesn't he? Ha! Don't be fooled! This cat's attitude is as sharp as his claws! He won't do anything unless there's something in it for him (except when I'm in trouble - which is often! - and then he's always there for me!). The big thing with Salem is that he's not really a cat. He's actually a warlock who the Witches' Council turned into a cat when he tried to take over the whole world!

HARVEY KINKLE

Harvey has always been in my life and I love him as my best friend. He knows I'm a witch, and he keeps it a secret…but he makes sure to stay on my good side because he knows that with one point I could turn him into a toad! (As if I would!)

JOSH

Another good friend of mine, Josh works at the *Boston Citizen* as a photographer. As you'll learn when you read my annual, he or Harvey might turn out to be my soulmate! (That's what's so great about life – you never know what's going to happen!)

ROXIE

One of my roommates, and a really close friend, even if she does think there's a cloud behind every silver lining! She's very pessimistic, but trying to cheer her up is half the fun. She's now a radio talk show host!

MORGAN

Another great roommate, Morgan is a little 'flighty' at the best of times, and her only interests are boys, fashion, boys, fashion and..um…boys! She's got a great future as a fashion designer!

My third roommate! Miles keeps us laughing – sometimes unintentionally. His idea of a dream date is a full-sized cardboard cutout of a famous actress. And he adamantly believes that many humans are actually Pod People in disguise! Told ya he's a little weird!

MILES

Sabrina The Teenage Witch™

The Gift of the Gab

Original story
written by
Bruce Ferber &
Marley Sims

Hey, fans! Guess which cool, handsome, kind'a debonair cat's gonna be telling you this juicy little story? Yeah, that's right – me, the King o' the Catnip himself…SALEM SABERHAGEN! And, who better to tell it, because, it's all about ME. (Okay, not all of it…but it should be!).

It all kicks off with my favourite teenage witch, Sabrina (don't worry, I'll get to ME in a moment!), who arrived back at her house at Adams College with some great news for her best friend, Roxie.

"The most incredible thing happened today," Sabrina announced excitedly, bursting into their living room. "The campus radio station accepted our proposal. We got our own show!"

Roxie stared at her, dumbfounded.

"We are so dead," she groaned. "How are we going to fill two hours, three nights a week?"

Sabrina was determined to remain upbeat.

"Roxie, we have tons of things to talk about. You and I lead really exciting lives."

She glanced around at her housemate Miles. He was apologizing to a life-sized cardboard cut-out of a famous film actress for having spilled grape juice on her.

"Okay," said Sabrina. "We've got two days to get really exciting lives."

Now we come to the best part – ME! (Hey, I'm not vain, I'm just honest!) Anyway, back at my house, Sabrina's Aunt Zelda and Aunt Hilda had discovered at a large, forlorn-looking dog sitting outside the front door.

"It's so cute," squealed a delighted Hilda. "Can we keep it? Can we?"

9

Now Zelda and I don't see eye-to-eye on many things (mostly about me using her credit card!), but, if I had known what was going down, she'd have had my full support when she said, "Hilda, I'm sure the dog already has an owner. We absolutely cannot… "

It was then the hairy mutt played its ace. It lifted its paw and tilted its head, as if begging for love.

" …let this precious creature perish on the street," she added quickly. "Come in, poochie!"

Rats! By the time I came out of the kitchen, the dog had already made itself at home.

"He's a dog!" I yelped, upon seeing it. "He'll rip me to shreds, skin me alive, gut me like a… "

The dog started to lick me. "Oh, work it, big guy," I purred. Look, you get licked and see how you can refuse!

They were overjoyed that pooch and I were getting along so well.

"I'll bet they'd like to share a pot roast," said Zelda, hurrying to the kitchen with Hilda.

Yowser! That'd never happened before! "Hallelujah!" I cried happily. "This could work out after all, bro."

The dog put his face right up against mine. "You are pretty cute," I decided. "I wonder what we should call you?"

The dog sneered. "Your worst nightmare!" it growled.

Now, while my life was flashing before my eyes, Sabrina's career as a DJ had hit a few bumps of its own!

Sitting alongside Roxie in the campus radio station booth, "Chick Chat" as they'd called their show (Eeeeuuuuh!) was hitting the airwaves for the first time – and was also hitting a few problems! Neither Sabrina nor Roxie could think of anything to chat about!

"So," said Sabrina, nervously speaking into the microphone. "What's on your mind, Roxie?"

Roxie, equally nervous, just shrugged her shoulders. "I don't know. What's on yours?"

Sabrina froze! "Well…uh…lots of stuff…you know…how 'bout we, uh," she stammered. "Kick things off with some dope jams?"

She punched a button and music began to play.

"Man," she gasped. "Talking on the radio is a little harder than I thought. We'll get the hang of it. We just need to chill with the trance, and then we'll be freestylin'!"

Roxie gave her a stony look.

"I downloaded some jargon off the internet," Sabrina said, weakly.

You thought that was tough? Try living with a mutt who was evil incarnate!

Not only did he hog the whole pot roast, Zelda and Hilda wouldn't even believe me when I told them that he could talk, and had admitted to me that he was a lowlife from the…Other Realm! (Shudder!)

It didn't help matters that this useless lump of fur was kissing up to them – literally. Hilda even suggested a name for him – Baby! ('Scuse me while I throw-up a hairball! "ACCK!")

If they only knew what I knew. For instance, when I took a much needed break in my litter box, I encountered something other than it's usual contents – the hard way!

"Who would be so demented as to put a mousetrap in my private sanctuary?" I hissed angrily.

"Howdy doody!" said you-know-who.

"All right," I snarled, flinging off the mousetrap while glaring daggers at the dog. "Cards on the table. Why are you here?"

"To sponge off those two daffy broads," admitted the dog.

"That's my racket, mac," I reminded him.

The dog smiled. "Not for long, pallie. And the name is Phil. I'm gonna get the broads to give you the boot, unless you choose to leave of your own free will."

"That is never going to happen," I snorted. "Now if you'll excuse me, I'm going outside to complete some unfinished business."

Still smarting, I leapt through the cat door…and my face met a stone wall. THUNK!

"Glad I went for the granite," sniggered Phil.

"Of course," I hissed, my face flattened. "You realise, this means war."

Back at the radio station, things had improved…but not for Sabrina!

After the first nerve-ridden programme, Roxie had suddenly hit her stride, and was hitting the airwaves like a pro.

Listeners were bombarding the station to talk to her!

Sabrina's attempts to chat naturally had fallen as flat as the index cards she had been using to prompt her about different subjects

Returning to the house, Roxie's words of encouragement sounded more to Sabrina like criticism. "Miles though it would help if I were prepared. Now you're telling me 'be spontaneous.' Well, I'm not listening to either of you," Sabrina announced.

"If you're not going to prepare and you're not going to be spontaneous, what does that leave?" Roxie asked.

Sabrina stormed into her room. "Wouldn't you like to know?" she said, closing the door. Then, under her breath, she groaned. "Wouldn't I like to know?!"

* * *

Meanwhile, my 'revenge-is-sweet' scheme sort'a fell flat thanks to Zelda's interfering! Phil – or The Bloated Beast, as I liked to call him – was snoozing at the foot of the piano.

So I accidentally on purpose, pushed a vase off the piano, hoping it would crack him a good one!

The vase fell...and then froze in mid-air!

"Salem Saberhagen, how could you do that to poor Baby?" spluttered an angry Zelda, who had stopped the vase's freefall with a point of her finger.

No matter how much I protested that Phil was trying to bump me off, it fell on deaf ears, and the next moment Zelda was tossing me outta my own house! Can you believe that?!! Phil was lapping it up!

Well, whenever I need a shoulder to cry on, there's only one place to go.

Unfortunately, arriving on the windowsill of her bedroom

window, I found Sabrina as much in the dumps as I was!

"You picked the wrong shoulder," she told me miserably. "I'm making a fool of myself on the radio while Roxie sits back and wows everybody."

For someone so bright, sometimes Sabrina can be very dim! "You seem to have forgotten," I reminded her. "You're a witch."

Hey, just call me genius!
Sabrina pointed

Sabrina the Teenage Witch 13

and FOOSH! In her hand appeared a box. A set of magical chattering teeth floated up from the box into the air.

"Give me a subject," said the teeth. "I start gabbing."

This is just what Sabrina needed!

After she had tested the teeth out on a few subjects, I gave it my own challenge. "How would you get revenge on someone whose mission it was to destroy you?" I asked.

"I'm just the Gift of the Gab," said the teeth, and then started incanting "When you're desperate to get even, call upon my good friend Steven."

The teeth sparkled and POOF!, a good-looking man in a suit appeared in Sabrina's bedroom.

"Let me guess," said Sabrina. "Even Steven."

I leapt into Steven's arms. Let's go do in the dog."

Later that afternoon, I was at home in the kitchen, keeping out of the mutt's way, when the phone rang. "Yello," I said, answering it. KAA-BOOM! The phone exploded, leaving me with a smoking head!

"Ouch," I said, whiskers singed.

Then Phil entered, sneering. "Tsk-tsk," he sniggered, looking at my fur-fried face. "Don't you know smoking stunts your growth? I am good."

As he left, I blew ash off myself and looked heavenward. "Steven," I hissed. "Ready to get even…"

Moments later, Zelda and Hilda were fussing over Phil – as usual! Zelda stopped momentarily to answer the ringing doorbell. She was delighted to find Steven waiting on the doormat.

"Well, hello," she said, dreamily.

"My name is Steven Evenson," said Steven, smiling. "I think you may have my dog." He showed Zelda a picture of Phil.

"Oh, my," groaned Zelda. "It certainly does look like him."

She invited him in and explained to situation to Hilda.

"You can't have him, buster," growled Hilda defensively. "Get out!" She turned to Zelda, "It can't be his dog. Baby doesn't even recognise him."

Steven looked at Phil. "Maybe it isn't him. And even if it is, he seems to be happier here. He was never really comfortable living in a forty-two room mansion with his own valet, the rich food at the country club, those luxurious sails on the yacht…"

Phil's ears perked up at this! He rushed

over to Steven and started licking him.

"He seems to know you now," said Hilda, disappointed.

"Yes, he does," said Steven. "But I have to do what's best for him. I'm leaving the dog with you."

Unable to stop himself, Phil shouted out, "Don't leave me with these losers! One's dumb as dirt, the other's got a personality of a limp noodle."

Da-dah! As Steven had planned, Phil's secret was out!

"Salem was right," gasped Hilda. "That dog was just using us."

I grinned. "Stick with the User you know," I said.

Steven handed the Aunts his business card. "I'm here to take this slobbering slimeball to Other Realm Obedience School."

A terrified Phil begged the Aunts to let his stay. They looked at each other and pointed. "Buh-bye," they said, and Phil and Steven disappeared! I'd won!!

At the radio station, the Gift of the Gab magic teeth weren't helping Sabrina. To both Roxie and the listeners' growing disbelief, she was talking non-stop nonsense – even in Japanese!

"Asoko wa yap'pari ii'naa, sakana shinsen de min-na mo iiyatsu ja'naa," she said, to a caller's question about Japanese restaurants.

"Could you say that in English, please?" asked the irate caller.

"There's a simply marvellous place downtown," said Sabrina, talking in a very posh English accent. "Where the fish is tip-top."

Sabrina could see Roxie staring at her, horrified.

"Man, I am bad at this," groaned Sabrina,

slipping out the teeth while Roxie wasn't looking.

"Spellman," said Roxie, annoyed. "What do you think you're doing?"

Sabrina shrugged. "Trying to be something I'm not. I'm not cut out to be on the radio, and nothing I do is going to magically change that."

She announced, live on air, that she was quitting the show! The phones lit up!

"It's my pleasure," said Sabrina. "To leave you in the very capable hands of the witty and talented, Roxie King!"

She smiled, giving Roxie the thumbs up!

* * *

As for me, life was a blast! Trying to make up for the way they'd treated me, Zelda and Hilda were feeding me the finest foods…and they'd made me a deluxe litter box. It had windows, a skylight and even a satellite dish!

"I'm so happy," I said, choking back tears. "I could…hmm, I think I will…"

I hopped into the litter box, and closed the curtains. It was sheer

To Many Salems!

I sure taught that Other Realm pooch that when it comes to cats, there's only one Salem Saberhaen! Meeoow!

How many times can you find my name in this word search grid? My name can be found vertically, horizontally and even diagonally!

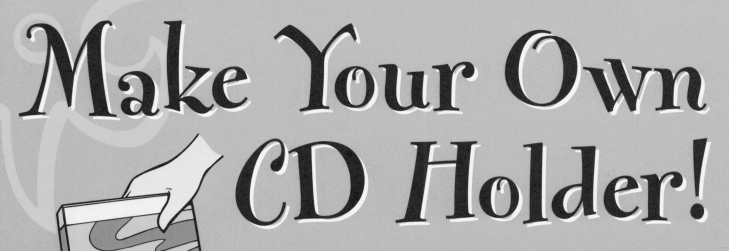

Make Your Own CD Holder!

Hi gang! Well, my attempt to be a DJ was a complete disaster! Oh, well, I can't be good at everything. To show Roxie there are no hard feelings, I made her a Salem CD holder to keep her CDs in order at the radio station – and now you can make one, too!

You will need from a craft shop

Two sheets of stiff card 3mm thick

4 polystyrene balls sized 40mm

2 wobbly cat's eyes

Some plastic straws, glue, sellotape, poster paint and felt tip pens (colours of your choice), scissors, tracing paper and pencil, and a small ball of plasticine.

How to Make

(Ask an adult for help when using sharp instruments)

1. Cut card to the shape and dimensions indicated (see diagram below). Using scissors, carefully score lines where shown.

2. Draw holes large enough for straws to be pushed through. With a piece of plasticine under each hole, push a pencil through the holes until they are big enough to take the straws.

3. Bend the card on the score lines and both glue and sellotape corners. Cut straws to length (156mm) and push through the holes. Use a small amount of glue on each hole to hold straws in place.

4. Glue a polystyrene ball to each corner on your holder to act as Salem's paws.

5. Trace the cat face onto the second sheet of card and cut out. Paint it black, if you want it to look like Salem, or any other colour you choose.

6. Glue the cat face onto the front of your holder.

7. Stick on cat's eyes. Decorate holder to your own design with poster paints, glitter or sticky shapes.

Just Joking

Zelda's always telling me to take my spells more seriously... but I'm a witch who just wants to have fun! Anyway, here are some of my favourite witch jokes – hope you like them!

Sabrina The Teenage Witch™

Salem: Meow!

Phil the dog: Moo!

Salem: What do you mean, 'moo'?

Phil: I'm learning a foreign language!

First Witch: What's your new boyfriend like?

Second Witch: He's mean, nasty, ugly, smelly and totally evil - but he has some bad points, too!

Aunt Zelda: What's the most important thing to remember in chemistry?

Aunt Hilda: Never lick the spoon!

Sabrina: Why don't ghosts make good witches?

Harvey: You can see right through their magic!

Sabrina: What's a Witch's favourite subject?

Aunt Zelda: Spelling!

Sabrina: How does a witch doctor ask a girl out on a date?

Salem: Voodoo like to go out with me?

Murder on the Halloween Express

Original story written by Dan Berendsen

Murder?? Yes, and it all started at my Aunts house!

We were all in the kitchen, tasting Aunt Zelda's Halloween taffy. I was grumbling about nowhere to go on Halloween Night.

"Uck! Why does Aunt Zelda always go so heavy on the unicorn?" I moaned, spitting the taffy back into its wrapper. Not seeing the trash can around, I absent-mindedly put it into my jacket pocket.

Salem showed me a flyer he'd been reading. "'For fabulous food and sophisticated fun, this mystery train is number one'," I read aloud. "Salem, this is perfect."

Salem hoped I'd take him along, but I wanted to spend Halloween with my friends.

"I had my heart set on riding the rails," he said, sounding really upset.

I smiled, pointing at him. "No reason you can't do that."

Next moment, he flew to the top of the banister and slid down the rail.

"Wheeee! One more time!" he chuckled.

It's a shame my friends weren't as thrilled with the Mystery Train ride as Salem was.

That night, at the station, we boarded an old diesel train, and filed into a dingy, empty car.

"Ooh, good thing you

paid in advance," said Roxie, oozing sarcasm. "We'll be lucky to find a place to sit."

Josh, who had complained non-stop about my Halloween plan, moaned that the car was freezing, and Miles was worried about the carcinogens in diesel smoke!

Luckily, the steward, dressed in an old-fashioned, grey railroad outfit, arrived before Harvey could have his say.

"Welcome aboard the Halloween Mystery Train, where murder is our business and our business is murder," he announced in a suitably chilling voice, while handing out peanuts and a juice box.

Except Josh didn't get any juice. One more thing for him to complain about.

"Here, take mine," I said, stopping him in mid-rant. I took my hand out of my pocket and found taffy stuck to my glove. Great.

> "Welcome aboard the Halloween Mystery Train, where murder is our business and our business is murder,"

"Having a little taffy emergency," I said, heading for the restroom. "I've got to go de-goo."

And it was while I was there that I overheard the conductor blowing his whistle.

"All aboard!" he shouted. "The Other Realm Express is now leaving the station!"

Other Realm Express!? Oh, no!! I had to get everyone off before...but it was too late. I quickly opened the restroom door to discover the passenger car had been magically transformed to a beautiful parlour car of the 1920's.

Okay, so the sofas, potted palms and a bar looked a whole lot nicer than those rows of ratty seats, and all my friends were actually kind of cool in period dress. But, this was so not good.

* * *

Things just sort'a went downhill from there. I tried to explain to the steward that there were mortals on board, but he said the only way to stop the train was to solve the mystery.

"You're the detective," he explained. He pointed a finger and I was suddenly dressed in a trench coat and fedora hat. I looked out of the window and saw the train flying in the air through thick London fog.

"May I present Countess Admira and her maid, Hortense," the steward said, and up stood Morgan, elegantly dressed and coifed. Beside her was Roxie in a dowdy maid's uniform, holding a feather duster.

"Delighted," said Morgan the Countess, shaking my hand. "I find modern travel so exhilarating, don't you?"

Then I was introduced to Miles, now better known as German Professor Augustine Von Claptrap, and to Biff Buffington – I mean, Harvey! – the international tennis star.

But where was Josh?

"You mean world renowned photographer, Kip Kodak,"

said the steward. "Unfortunately, he's been a victim of..."

A loud THUD! behind us made us all turn. Josh was lying still on the floor.

"...murder," finished the steward.

Panicking, I knelt down to feel Josh's pulse. There was none. He really was...dead!

"And the game begins," cackled the steward. "All you have to do is figure out which one of our passengers killed Kip Kodak."

I stared dumbstruck at my friends. They all turned away, looking guilty...!

I gave solving the case my best shot! (Which wasn't much, considering I couldn't even beat my Aunts at "Clue"!)

First I interviewed Morgan.

"Everyone is so preoccupied with murder," the 'Countess' complained. "What you should be focused on is what happened to my ring. The hundred carat Star of Paramus is missing!"

She held out her hand. Her ring was missing a giant stone.

I interrogated her further and discovered that she and Josh – Kip, whatever! – had been madly in love, until he ended the affair. She vowed she'd get her revenge!

"But then I got over it and we became friends," she said brightly.

"So, I really have no motive for killing him."

Nope. None whatsoever.

The others had equally strong motives.

The maid Hortense (Roxie – keep up with me people!) hated the Countess and would have loved to have framed her for murder, but, of course, wouldn't admit if she had. Miles/Professor Claptrap, nervously cleaned his pipe with a pipe cleaner, and let it slip that he hated Kip Kodak for his success with women.

"He vas ze kind of guy who makes guys like me blend into ze wallpaper!" he snapped angrily. Then he changed his tone and calmly claimed, "I really have no motive vatsoever."

Biff 'Harvey' Buffington hated Kip for stealing his woman.

"I used to be in love with a woman. A wonderful, magical woman," he said. " And that

> "What you should be focused on is my ring. The hundred carat Star of Paramus is missing!"

scoundrel stole her from me."

"Let me guess," I sighed. " You had no motive whatsoever."

After finishing the interrogations, I went to see the spooky steward, who wanted to know what I'd come up with.

"First, your play involves a lot of ham acting," I told him. " Second, I have no idea who killed Kip."

He suggested darkly that I should find out. "What happens if I don't?"

He grinned, and a chill ran down my back.

"Unless you solve this case," he hissed. " You and your mortal friends will be trapped on this train…forever."

Right. No pressure then.

"This is insane," I complained, following the steward around the cabin. " We can't just go soaring through the cosmos forever."

"I'm sorry," he said huffily. "But rules are rules. Besides, everything you need to solve the crime is right in front of you."

"Right in front of me where?" I asked as I tripped over Josh's body. I always forget how literal witches are.

"He's still holding the juice box I gave him," I gasped. "And it's unopened. "That means he was killed right after I left him."

In his other hand, he was holding…the Countess's missing diamond!

I'd found the murderer!! Well, maybe not because I also discovered an old sweaty towel beneath the body, embroidered with the initials 'B.B.'. Biff Buffington perhaps? First I had no clues, now I had too many clues! This was not going to be easy…!

While this little drama was being played out, my Aunts had discovered that Salem had sent me on an Other Realm Mystery Train. They were rushing to my rescue with the cat in tow!

The three of them were waiting on an empty train platform somewhere in the cosmos, a beautiful field of stars surrounding them.

"According to the timetable," said Aunt Zelda. "The train left Boston two hours ago."

"There it is now!" shouted Aunt Hilda, as the train flew past. "But it's not stopping. What are we going to do?"

There was only one thing they could do! "Jump!" yelled Aunt Zelda, leaping off the platform!

"So, let's go through what we know so far." I paced the cabin, trying my hardest to act like a world's greatest detective. " I exited the cabin and Kip was alive. I came back and Kip was dead. That's about it."

Suddenly, the cabin door banged open and in staggered my Aunts. "Thank goodness you're here," I cried, rushing up to them. "I had no idea this was an Other Realm train."

Then I noticed they were rather sooty and windblown. "Did somebody shoot you guys out of a cannon?"

My Aunts pointed at themselves. With a flash of magic, they were transformed into clean, period clothing. Aunt Zelda laid out the plan. "Okay, first I'll go and interrogate the steward. He knows who the murderer is. We'll have it out of him ten minutes tops."

"Five if he's ticklish," grinned Aunt Hilda.

"And if that doesn't work," chimed in Salem. "You always have me to solve the crime. At least you would, if I had the appropriate attire."

Aunt Zelda pointed at Salem. BING! Now he was dressed like Sherlock Holmes, complete with pipe!

"I say, good show, old girl," said Salem, in a very English voice. " Now then, what say we have a look at the corpse, shall we?"

And give the cat credit, moments later he had solved the murder!

"This body is simply rife with clues," he snorted, giving me a withering look. "What, pray tell, have you been doing for the last few hours?"

"Hey, I found the diamond and the towel," I muttered defensively.

"Hmm," pondered the Great Cat Detective. "Those items combined with this feather I found." He held up a large feather from beneath the body. "Tell us everything we need to know."

Seems the crime went something like this...!

* * *

While I was out of the cabin, the Countess, who had planned to murder Kip, offered her hand for him to kiss, knowing that the prong on her ring was loose.

The giant diamond came off and lodged in Kip's throat. He started choking, and the Countess would have gotten away with murder if Hortense hadn't stepped in!

Even though she wanted Kip dead, her instincts as a former RAF nurse got the better of her. She grabbed him around the waist and squeezed him tightly so he coughed up the diamond. Luckily, according to Salem, Hortense still had her feather duster...and a plan.

"She knew Kip was highly allergic to emu feathers," said Salem, staring at Roxie accusingly. "And that prolonged exposure could kill him."

Aha! I thought. Hortense is the murderer! But, no, she wasn't. The feathers from the duster did go up Kip's nose, but he

sneezed, dislodging all but one from his nostrils.

That's apparently when Biff Buffington seized upon the opportunity to kill Kip himself, and offered him one of his towels.

"To wipe his nose...or to strangle him?!" demanded Salem, glaring at Biff.

"I didn't," said Biff, acting the innocent.

Salem had to agree. The accusation was just cat was just being melodramatic. Then Salem said he had found pipe smoke on the body...and the only person who smokes a pipe is Professor Claptrap! The Professor had offered Kip his pipe to calm his nerves.

Everyone knows that tobacco can kill you. "But Kip doesn't smoke," I reminded him.

"Exactly," deduced Salem Holmes. "Which is why the Professor is definitely not the murderer!"

AAAAAGGGHH! Sometimes that cat drives me nuts!

Well, we had a body, so someone had to be the murderer. Salem began his final recap of events by going back to me eating Aunt Zelda's taffy in the kitchen.

"The murder was committed by someone who had motive and means," intoned Salem. "Someone who had a working knowledge of poison, who knew that in large quantities, essence of unicorn is fatal to mortals..."

And disgusting in taffy, I thought. Especially when the taffy then gets stuck to your glove.

"Someone," continued Salem. "Who knew that the poison need not be ingested, but can easily be absorbed through the skin. And placed on something as innocuous…"

Oh no! I suddenly knew where this was going.

"…as a juice box!"

The murderer was…me??! I had apparently taken the taffy off of my glove and stuck it to the box before I handed the juice to Josh.

Salem deduced my motive was that I was angry with Josh for not being more supportive of my manic quest for the perfect Halloween. So a rage built up inside of me…and I killed Josh!

Gotta admit, I totally didn't see that one coming. "Well," said the steward, appearing with my Aunts. "Now that you've solved the murder, you're free to get off the train."

"Wow. This was great," I said. You sure throw a nice homicide. But how did you know about Aunt Zelda's taffy and that I was mad at Josh?"

"Murder is out business," the steward reminded me. "And our business is murder. Last stop, Boston!"

The train changed back to its normal shabby state, and everyone, including Josh, returned to normal, with no memory of what had happened.

"Wow," I chuckled to Salem. "He really does murder right."

It's Murder!

Boy, I'm not much good as a detective – I didn't even figure out that I was the murderer!! Can you unjumble the words below to spell out six ways of being murdered? Each word has an extra letter, which will spell out a seventh way to die!

1 NGGAINHS

2 LNXSPOIEOO

3 BBGINTSAN

4 NORGPIWDN

5 IWUONRND

6 TONGOHSOI

ANSWERS: 1 – Hanging, 2 – Explosion, 3 – Stabbing, 4 – Drowning, 5 – Rundown, 6 – Shooting.
The seventh way to be murdered is....Poison!

29

Spelling Lessons!

Sabrina's not the only one who can cast spells – here are some of my own favourites! (Oh, okay, they're not really magic, but I can pretend, can't I? Try them out on your friends!)

Magic Ring

Tell your friends that you are going to turn a paper ring into a much larger one by, of all things, cutting it in half!

To perform this trick you will need a pair of blunt-ended scissors and a large paper ring made from a paper strip stuck together. Hold up the paper ring to your friends, and tell them you are going to cut it in two to make two rings. This done, hold the two halves in one hand.

Open out the two halves and say a magic word. Magically, you've turned the two halves into a much larger single paper ring!

The trick is to make one twist in the original paper strip before sticking the ends together!

Magic Water Trick

This trick uses water, so make sure you perform it either outside in the garden or over the sink!

You will need

Two sheets of stiff card 3mm thick

4 polystyrene balls sized 4

2 identical large plastic beakers

Enough warm – not HOT! – water to fill one beaker

Enough cold water to fill the other beaker

A postcard

Food colouring

Completely fill one beaker with the warm water, the other with cold water. Add some food colouring to the beaker with the warm water. Hold the postcard on top of that glass, making sure it's large enough not to allow the water to spill out.

Turn the beaker over, placing it so its rim is touching that of the beaker of cold water. (This might get messy the first few times of practising, so make sure you're wearing old clothes!) Remove the card. The coloured water still remains in the top beaker.

Carefully turn the two beakers once over, so that the cold water beaker is now on top. The coloured water will rise to the top again! (This is because warm air rises!)

Are You a Gr

How good a detective are you? Can you find all the words listed on the right in the word grid, either vertically, horizontally or diagonally? Each word is one of a pair. Can you match them up? (For instance, 'Kodak' and 'Kip' when paired become Kip Kodak!)

```
G R E E N W
S T R V E N
D D K A Y L
E S I B L K
V U N E A M
E S G D Y R
N E O B O I
S K D X E A
O O I L D P
N E G A H R
```

eat Detective?

1) One word is shown twice. Which one is it? **2)** the leftover letters will spell out a place Sabrina visits in the story 'I, Busybody'. Do you know what it is? Time yourself to see how fast you can solve this great detective puzzle!

```
I  C  H  B
O  K  U  E
T  I  S  G
H  P  P  A
E  B  L  L
R  S  E  L
M  O  M  I
Y  S  H  V
K  I  N  G
E  B  A  S
```

- KIP
- KING
- ADAMS
- OTHER
- KODAK
- REALM
- ROXIE
- SALEM
- STEVEN
- COLLEGE
- EVENSON
- VILLAGE
- GREENWICH
- SABERHAGEN

ANSWERS: 1) ADAMS COLLEGE, GREENWICH VILLAGE, KIP KODAK, OTHER REALM, ROXIE KIND, SALEM SABERHAGEN, STEVEN EVENSON 2) KING, 3) BUDDY'S BUSY BODY SHOP

Sabrina and the Candidate

Original story written by Jon Vandergriff

Hey, gang! You know how much I want to be a journalist when I finish college? Well, thanks to Josh putting in a good word for me with his editor, I'm now an intern at the *Boston Citizen* newspaper!

But don't get too excited. It's not like I'm hanging out with famous celebs or writing story exclusives. I'm more your 'take down notes and make the coffee' sort of reporter at the moment…

Or at least I was, before the city council elections came around and I suddenly found myself shouting, "Hold the front page!".

Every story needs a beginning, and ours starts at Aunt Hilda's Coffee House, where Aunt Zelda was canvassing votes to get politician Robert Russell elected city councilman.

"Robert Russell is an encyclopedia on the ins and outs of local government," she told the large crowd gathered around the voter registration table. "No one is better informed on the issues."

Or better looking, if the swooning women in the room were any indication. Robert Russell may have been smart and informed, but he was also a serious hunk.

Aunt Hilda thought so too, and was

loving the fact that the crowd was knocking back her coffee while they waited for him to speak.

"I just raised the price to four-fifty a cup," she told me conspiratorially, as I stood there making notes to give my editor. My Aunt, the entrepreneur!

The crowd burst into applause when Russell began to speak. He promised that if he were elected, he would fight for the district, and protect the citizens from senseless price-gouging. The crowd applauded even louder. "I love this guy," said Aunt Hilda.

Russell held up one of her coffee cups. "For example," he continued. "Why should you have to pay four-fifty for a cup of coffee?"

"I hate this guy," said Aunt Hilda.

When I got back to the offices of the *Boston Citizen*, I went over over the poll numbers with Josh and our editor, Mike.

"According to this poll," Josh was telling us. "Russell has eighty-four percent of the vote."

"I'm not surprised," I piped up, my mouth working faster than my brain. "When you see him in person, you understand why everyone thinks he's so hot." Oops! "I mean, politically astute. Objectively speaking, of course."

Mike handed me a photocopied picture. "You might want to check out the latest candidate to join the race. My heart sank. I was looking at a picture of Aunt Hilda. Beneath her face was a caption: "Hilda Spellman For City Council."

It had to be a joke. She didn't know anything about politics!

Unfortunately, it wasn't. Out of spite for his remark about her coffee, Aunt Hilda was determined to bring Robert Russell down. Her campaign slogan? "He dissed me. Now let's diss him back."

Aunt Zelda and I tried desperately to get her to stop her crazy plan, but she wouldn't listen. Especially when Salem arrived back at my Aunts' house to say he'd dug up dirt on Russell. He'd seen him with some shady characters!

I was so not impressed. "I can see the headline now. 'Talking Cat Sees Shady Characters.' Aunt Hilda, there is no story here."

But she wouldn't give up. And rather than her running an unsubstantiated rumour about Russell, I agreed, unwillingly, to investigate.

It turned out there was more to Salem's suspicions than I thought!

> As all good investigative journalists are trained to do, we hunkered down in the trash can and peered into the house.

* * *

Aunt Zelda and I went to Russell's house to check out Salem's story. The cat came along for the ride, or maybe, the garbage. As all good investigative journalists are trained to do, we hunkered down in the trash can and peered into the house.

At first all we saw was Russell reading a bedtime story to his six year old daughter. No big expose there! But just as we were about to leave, Russell hustled his daughter out of the room, and returned with one of Salem's 'shady characters'.

"I can't see what they're doing," complained Aunt Zelda.

Which, being witches, wasn't a problem.

Some quick finger-pointing and she and I appeared in the room as the two dolls Russell's daughter had been holding.

"Wow," I said, looking down at myself wearing a beautiful doll's dress. "I've never been a big fan of gingham, but this totally works."

"Maybe for you," muttered Aunt Zelda, squirming uncomfortably. "But my bloomers are stitched to my waist."

We watched as Russell took several hundred-dollar bills from his wall safe. I pointed to myself and a miniature camcorder appeared around my neck. I wanted all this on tape!

"You know the drill," Russell was telling the other guy, stuffing the money into unmarked envelopes. "Deliver these to the appropriate constituents and not a word about who they're from."

"Omigod!" I squeaked. "Robert Russell is buying votes!"

"Salem was right," gasped Aunt Zelda. "He is a slimeball." She started to cry.

"Oh, Aunt Zelda," I said, sympathetically. "I know you're disappointed, but don't cry."

"I can't help it," she blubbered. "I'm a Baby Cries-A-Lot!"

Well, everything hit the fan after I showed my editor the tape. Especially after he recognised Russell's companion as an ex-convict.

On the front cover of next day's edition of the *Boston Citizen*, above my first-ever journalistic byline, screamed the headline: "Would-Be Councilman Bankrolls Ex-Con. Russell Responds With No Comment."

Aunt Hilda was delighted. Thanks to me the polls showed she'd taken Russell's eighty-four percent lead in the council elections.

"Sabrina, I'm going to be Westbridge's next councilwoman," she trilled, when Aunt Zelda and I met her at the coffee house. "And it's all thanks to you."

"Aunt Hilda," I snapped. "I wrote that piece because people have the right to know the truth. Not to help someone who's completely unqualified for the job."

Miles had been reading the paper at the next table and wondered what Russell was hiding. Zelda just didn't want to know. Which worked out well, because I didn't have a clue!

"Isn't it your job to find out?" purred Aunt Hilda.

GURRRR!!

Trouble is, she was right.

As a reporter, I needed

envelope to a rundown apartment building. I was about to uncover the sleazy little scheme Russell was up to!

Inside the apartment I could see a poorly dressed, harassed-looking mother with three hungry children.

"Thank you so much," she said to Louie, when he handed her one of the envelopes. "I've been out of work for three months and I didn't know how I was going to pay my rent."

Perhaps "sleazy" was an overstatement.

The mother asked where the money had come from, but Louie told her the donor wished to remain anonymous. "But I can tell you this," he said. "That man is a saint."

Omigod! I wrote a scathing article about a saint??

"He's more than a saint," said the woman, choking back the tears. "He's an angel."

And I'd just lopped off his wings!

My career as an investigative journalist looked to be over before it had even begun!

My first words to Mike when I got to the newspaper were, "Russell isn't buying votes. He's giving money to the poor. You have to run a retraction."

His to me were, "I can't run a retraction. First off, you didn't bring me any proof. Secondly, I just called Russell again, and he still said 'no comment'."

to see the story through to the end.

So back I went to Russell's house, this time alone, arriving in time to watch through the window as Russell stuffed more money into unmarked envelopes, for another shady-looking character called Louie.

"It's time to find out where that cash is headed," I decided. I pointed a finger and POP! My face appeared on one of the bills Russell was holding, wearing a powdered wig and period clothes and looking a lot like Ben Franklin.

"Wow. I am so money," I thought.

Louie carried me in an

It didn't make sense! He was doing incredibly generous things for people – why would he hide that?

"Good question," agreed Mike. "If I wanted the answer, who could get it for me? Let's see... this is a newspaper... I've got it. Someone who wants to be a reporter. Sabrina, do you know anybody?"

It took a second for the penny to drop. He meant me!

Naturally, Robert Russell was in no mood to talk, especially to me. He tried to slam the door in my face, but being a witch, that never works. I pointed a finger and the door sprang back open.

"Why would I talk to you of all people?" he demanded.

"Because I unfairly damaged your reputation and now I want to help you," I admitted, feeling even worse about myself.

"Sabrina, I gave the money anonymously because I wanted to help people and give them a second chance," Russell told me after finally letting me in. "But I didn't want anyone thinking I was buying votes."

Ouch.

He agreed to go on record about his charitable work, but he understandably refused to give me the names of the people he had been helping out.

"I want to

> Naturally, Robert Russell was in no mood to talk, especially to me. *He tried to slam the door in my face, but being a witch, that never works.*

respect their privacy," he said.

"Hey, if there's one reporter who understands respecting privacy, it's me." I said.

Russell gave me a stony glare.

"Starting now."

The next edition of the *Boston Citizen* ran the headline, 'Russell Says Money is Gift for the Poor'.

That should have done the trick. Humans being what they are, it didn't. He stayed well down in the polls against Aunt Hilda.

"It's always easier to destroy a reputation than to build one back up," Aunt Zelda reminded me. I felt awful.

Back at my house, I looked up 'restoring reputations' spells on my laptop.

"To clear the air and show he's great," I read out aloud. "Put him in a public debate."

Roxie burst into our room. "Sabrina, I just had the craziest idea. Let's set up a debate between Hilda and Russell and I can broadcast it on my radio show."

"That is crazy," I agreed. "So crazy it just might work."

A few days later, the great radio political debate was underway.

"This debate is exactly what Russell needs," Aunt Zelda said, as we sat in our seats with the rest of the audience that filled the college hall. "When people see how passionate he is about the issues, they'll be convinced of his integrity."

I chuckled. "All I can say is, I wouldn't want to be Aunt Hilda going up against him." At which moment, she appeared.

"Okay, here's the joke I thought I'd open with," she told us excitedly. "A priest, a rabbi and Camryn Manheim walk into a bar…"

"Like I said," I whispered to Aunt Zelda. "We have nothing to worry about."

And for once in this whole sorry mess, I was right!

"What do I think about multi-use re-zoning?" said Aunt Hilda, standing on stage at a podium facing Russell. Roxie was seated between them asking the questions. "I like it. Re-zoning, recycling, refried beans…Re-member me when you go to the polls!" The audience groaned.

"Working like a charm, Sabrina," said Aunt Zelda.

"Like taking candy from a baby," I chuckled.

Roxie was getting annoyed with Aunt Hilda's lack of seriousness.

"Ms. Spellman, so far you haven't told us any of your views on anything."

"Of course I haven't," beamed Aunt Hilda. "I'm a politician. Ba-dum-bum!"

from the *Boston Citizen*.

"I almost destroyed a man and I'm only an intern. Think of all the damage I'd do if I became a full-fledged reporter," I explained.

"You're being way too hard on yourself," he said. "Sometimes you make mistakes. If you really want to quit, I can't stop you." He paused. "Yes, I can. Don't be an idiot. You're good at this. Now get back to work."

Well, when he put it like that...!

We watched Robert Russell's landslide victory at my Aunts' house. He got 12,782 votes to Aunt Hilda's one. And that one vote was disqualified because it had been marked with a paw print instead of a signature.

"Hey, you try holding a pen with a dewclaw," Salem said.

Still, Aunt Hilda wasn't too upset. 99% of those who voted said she was the candidate they'd sooner play 'Twister' with. And we all agreed she had been a lot funnier than Russell.

"And that's going to be my ace in the whole when I run for governor," she told us. "Who's up for a game of 'Twister'?"

The audience began to boo.

I turned to Aunt Zelda, grinning. "That may have been the final nail in Aunt Hilda's political coffin."

And it was!

* * *

Still, I felt bad for all the trouble I'd caused, so I went to Mike and told him I was resigning

Don't be Cat'ty!

Salem here! All this fuss about elections – everyone should just vote for me! Anyway can you solve my cat puzzle? Each answer to the following questions begins with 'CAT'. The coloured line down the centre of the puzzle will spell out something Sabrina wants to become.

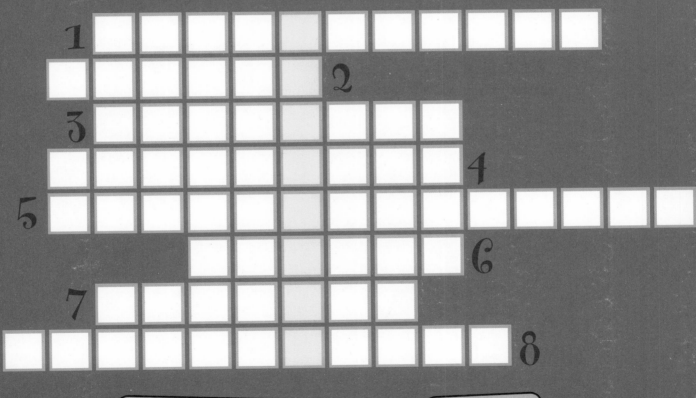

1 **Larvae of a butterfly or moth**

2 **Livestock**

3 **Slingshot**

4 **List of books, names etc in alphabetical order**

5 **Firework**

6 **Flowery spikes on willow tree**

7 **A boarding place for cats**

8 **Disaster**

ANSWERS: 1) CATERPILLAR, 2) CATTLE, 3) CATAPULT, 4) CATALOGUE, 5) CATHERINE WHEEL, 6) CATKIN, 7) CATTERY, 8) CATASTROPHE.
The hidden word is REPORTER.

Vote for Me!

LOCAL E[

True or False

1 Sabrina shares a house with Roxie, Morgan and Mike.

2 Aunt Zelda has been dating Professor Adams.

3 Harvey knows that Sabrina is a witch.

4 Aunt Zelda's ex-boyfriend Gabriel was a singer.

5 Aunt Hilda has been dating President Banning.

6 Miles believes in alien life forms.

7 Mike is the editor of the *Boston Times*.

Vote for Hilda

	TRUE	FALSE		TRUE	FALSE
	X		8	☐	☐
1	☐	☐	9	☐	☐
2	☐	☐	10	☐	☐
3	☐	☐	11	☐	☐
4	☐	☐	12	☐	☐
5	☐	☐	13	☐	☐
6	☐	☐	14	☐	☐
7	☐	☐	15	☐	☐

8) FALSE - FASHION DESIGNER, 9) TRUE, 10) FALSE - 'CHIK CHAT', 11) TRUE, 12) TRUE, 13) TRUE, 14) FALSE - MALE, 15) FALSE - PERU

44

Aunt Hilda and Aunt Zelda are battling it out in the local elections! But which candidate knows most about their constituents?

This is a game for two players. Flick a coin to see who will be Aunt Hilda or Aunt Zelda. Then take it in turns to see who can answer most questions right. The person with the most questions right wins the election!

ECTIONS

8 Morgan wants to be a famous model.

9 Sabrina goes to Adams College.

10 Roxie has a radio talk show called 'Chick Chat'.

11 Salem is an American shorthaired cat.

12 Sabrina's mother is named Diana.

13 Aunt Hilda owns a coffee shop.

14 A warlock is a female witch.

15 Sabrina's mom works on an archaeological dig in Palma.

Vote for Zelda

	TRUE	FALSE		TRUE	FALSE
1	X	☐	8	☐	☐
2	☐	☐	9	☐	☐
3	☐	☐	10	☐	☐
4	☐	☐	11	☐	☐
5	☐	☐	12	☐	☐
6	☐	☐	13	☐	☐
7	☐	☐	14	☐	☐
			15	☐	☐

ANSWERS: 1) FALSE - MILES, 2) FALSE - PROFESSOR CARLIN, 3) TRUE, 4) FALSE - POET, 5) TRUE, 6) TRUE 7) FALSE - THE BOSTON CITIZEN.

You're a Winner!

I voted for Sabrina's Aunt Hilda, even if no one else did…! But it's not only political candidates who like wearing rosettes. You could make you own for school elections, to give winners at sports day or your school fete – hey, you could even make one for yourself, and wear it with pride! After all, you're *always* a champ! Meow!

You will need

Small piece of paper. Small piece of card from a cereal box. 1.5m of coloured ribbon from craft shop. A stapler. Safety pin. Small piece of sellotape. Glue stick

How to Make

Cut the paper and card to a 65mm circle. Make two card circles. Form loops in ribbon (approx. 30mm loops – as an adult to help!), and staple them to the paper disc as you go.

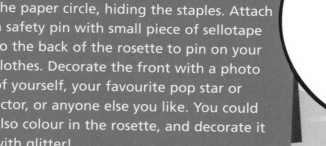

Stick the cardboard circles on both sides of the paper circle, hiding the staples. Attach a safety pin with small piece of sellotape to the back of the rosette to pin on your clothes. Decorate the front with a photo of yourself, your favourite pop star or actor, or anyone else you like. You could also colour in the rosette, and decorate it with glitter!

Deliver us from Email

Original story written by Dan Kael.

Harvey here. I've got a secret that I've never shared with anyone...I'm the only human who knows that Sabrina is really a witch! It really freaked me out at first, but I'm cool with it now. (I just make sure not to upset her too much since I know with one point she could turn me into a toad! Hey, Sabrina, I was joking – honest!)

But there was one time when knowing Sabrina was a witch helped me save her from a wicked witch's spell...! (And also taught me how dangerous it can be opening e-mails from people you don't know!)

Sabrina was doing her internship at the *Boston Citizen*. She was also trying to convince her editor, Mike, to let her write a regular column. She wanted to prove that she could do more than just make coffee and copies.

Mike is a tough, no-nonsense sort of guy, and making the pitch was far from easy.

"Okay, how about any of these?" said Sabrina desperately, handing Mike a piece of paper from her folder.

"I like them all," said Mike, reading down the list. Sabrina beamed.

"Unfortunately," he said. "I've read them all. Sabrina, you've got some really good instincts. And I've got the feeling that if you keep at it, you'll

come up with something."

"You're right," nodded Sabrina, pitching again. "College students: you give them a second chance and they'll come up with something!"

"Keep thinking," sighed Mike.

"College students," said Sabrina, pitching harder. "They keep thinking."

Mike pointed to the door. That was Sabrina's cue to scram.

While Sabrina was trying to create a career,

her Aunt Hilda was creating something else. I'm still not quite sure what it was, but it was a result of her new obsession with knitting.

"My new hobby is so relaxing," she told Salem, who was busy at his laptop computer.

"Maybe for you," he moaned. "But I'm trying to concentrate on expanding my intellectual horizons."

Hilda peered at the screen.

"'There once was a witch from Helsinki'...? Who's sending you this garbage?"

"NastyGirl at 'The-Slammer-Dot-Org'. Meow," blushed Salem.

And NastyGirl was also sending the same e-mails to Sabrina!

"I am so close to getting my own column for the newspaper," she muttered to Miles, as she worked on her laptop in the living room of their off-campus house. "I don't have time to deal with this."

She quickly replied to the e-mail. "'Dear Airhead. Stop harassing me with your annoying e-mails. They're nothing but mindless garbage.'" Then she hit the send button.

What Sabrina didn't know was that NastyGirl was really Katrina her evil twin who was locked up in an Other Realm prison cell!

"'Airhead'? 'Mindless garbage'?" she spluttered, upon receiving Sabrina's e-mail. "I may be an evil twin, but I still have feelings."

Katrina wasn't only evil, she was spiteful, so she decided to ruin Sabrina's life by e-mailing her a nasty computer virus!

"We'll see who's the airhead now," she cackled. "They say ignorance is bliss. Sabrina, you're about to be very, very happy."

Sabrina's computer announced the arrival of new mail.

"'Apologises from NastyGirl'" she read. "Good. I guess whoever it is got the message."

She hit a key to open the email. Her computer expanded and sneezed! AAA-CHOOOO!

"Whoa. What was that?" she wondered. Then she expanded and sneezed. AAA-CHOOO!

"That was, like, so weird," said Sabrina, not realising that she had caught an Other Realm computer bug!

But it was soon noticeable to everyone else!

Roxie came home from class with news. And it wasn't good.

"Adams is thinking of cutting scholarships by twenty-five percent," she said angrily.

"Whatever," shrugged Sabrina. "What would you think if I highlighted my eyebrows?"

Roxie stared at her. She had just told Sabrina something that could affect her whole future.

"And the colour of my eyebrows doesn't affect mine?" snapped Sabrina. "If I go one shade too dark it could, like, totally trash all the work I've done with my hair."

"What is going on with you?" demanded Roxie. "Did all your brains fall out of your head?"

Sabrina looked on the floor. "I don't see any brains," she said, picking up a coin.

"But I did find a nickel. Woo-hoo!"

Later, at the newspaper, Sabrina sat blowing bubble gum bubbles and filing her nails.

"Oh, hi Mikey," she said, when she saw Mike approaching.

"Mikey?" Her editor glared at her.

"It's a fun name for Mike," she explained.

"Right," Mike said, completely unamused. Despite her odd behaviour, Mike invited Sabrina to join the reporters at the conference table. "My staff tends to be a little better at the whole 'give-the-new-kid-a-break' thing," he admitted.

"Oh, I don't need a break yet,"

beamed Sabrina stupidly. "Maybe I'll take one after the meeting."

With Sabrina's brains temporarily unavailable, the meeting was a disaster. Her friend Josh was there, and stared in disbelief when Sabrina's idea of what she wanted to write about was,

"Guys"

Everyone glared at her.

"Where are all the cute guys on campus?" Sabrina demanded.

"You want to write about getting a cute boyfriend?" said Mike incredulously.

Someone sarcastically suggested that Sabrina's second column would be Ten Ways to Get Thinner Thighs!

"I like it. We should do that column first, though" Sabrina reasoned. "'Cause you'll never get a cute boyfriend with fat thighs."

Josh quickly ushered Sabrina out of the office.

"You've made a fool of yourself and a fool of me," he snapped. "I went out on a limb to get this job for you. What is wrong with you? Is there wind coming through your ears?

"Better than from somewhere else," giggled Sabrina. "I made a funny."

"Will you knock it off?" said Josh crossly. "This was your big shot and you blew it. You'll be lucky if they keep you as an intern."

Sabrina didn't seem to care. And she didn't like Josh being such a grump.

"How do you think I'd look with bangs?" she asked.

"I don't care how you'd look with bangs!" Josh snapped.

"That is so insensitive," said Sabrina, walking off. "Buh-bye."

Sabrina was in big trouble...!

* * *

I stopped by Sabrina's house later that day, and one look told me something was wrong.

"Sabrina, I'm no magic expert,"

game of touch your nose and balance on one foot, while saying 'Ahh'.

"This game is fun," she giggled. "Aunt Zelda, touch your elbow, put your leg around your neck and say 'wheee!'"

"I think she may have some sort of airhead virus," Zelda said. She looked to her sister for confirmation, but Hilda was focused entirely on her knitting. Zelda soon got Hilda's attention though. She gave me one end of a piece of yarn attached to Hilda's knitted pod. She took another end and we pulled.

Hilda spun around and around like the Tasmanian Devil! When she stopped spinning she was completely out of the pod.

"Wow! I guess I can skip spinning class today," she stammered, dizzily.

Peering into Sabrina's ears, her Aunts could see each other through her head.

"Just as I feared," said Zelda. "Sabrina's head is completely empty. This airhead virus has drained her of all her substance."

Zelda realized almost immediately that some unusual email had caused Sabrina's condition. Well, she does have like, twelve PhD's. Anyway, when she could finally get a straight answer from Sabrina she reasoned that it had to do with those emails coming from the Other Realm prison.

"Why would someone in an Other Realm prison want to hurt Sabrina?" I asked. "Who would be so evil?"

"Her Aunts stared at each other, gasping in recognition. Next thing I knew Zelda pointed at herself and disappeared...!

Turns out she went to the Other Realm prison and had it out with Katrina.

"There is no antidote," cackled Katrina. "You came all this way for nothing."

Katrina was immovable and truly evil. But luckily, she was also rooming with

I said. "But it looks to me like you're under a spell."

"Spell?" said Sabrina, looking dumb.

"You're a witch, remember?" I reminded her.

Sabrina grinned. "Oh, my gosh. That's right."

I needed to get Sabrina to her Aunts' house asap!

Her Aunt Hilda was still knitting. Every piece of furniture was covered in a knitted throw, and there was knitted stuff all over the floor. Hilda had even knitted herself into a woollen pod!

"I think Sabrina is under some kind of spell," I told her Aunt Zelda. "She's acting really weird."

As Zelda examined her, Sabrina played a

Jezebelda – Zelda's evil twin! And Jezebelda was as simple as Zelda was smart. So, all Zelda had to do was bribe her evil twin to get the answer: Sabrina had to relearn all of life's lessons. And she had to do it by daybreak the next day, or she would remain a pea-brain forever!

Zelda hurried back to Westbridge. "Okay, I've got the antidote," she said. Knowing it wouldn't be easy to keep Sabrina's attention, she came up with an interesting plan.

"It's time to play a little game," Zelda explained.

Great! Sabrina loved games!

Zelda continued, "This game is called "We Put Everything You Used to Know Back in Your Head, and You Commit it to Memory and Apply it to Every Waking Moment of Your Daily Life."

"Sabrina looked disappointed. "Can't we play 'Kerplunk'?" she asked.

"Maybe we should start simple," suggested Hilda, turning to Sabrina. "Do unto others as you would have others do unto you."

"A penny saved is a penny earned," I chimed in.

"Don't eat yellow snow," Salem reminded her.

And so it went on, hour after hour, cramming facts, figures and feelings back into Sabrina's head. By the time we finished, we were all exhausted, but Sabrina's head was full of knowledge again!

"Now you just have to be able to use it to get your life back in order," Zelda told her.

Which meant a lot of apologising and a lot of grovelling!

"Look, I just want to apologise for my

"Just as I suspected, Sabrina's head is completely empty. This airhead virus has drained her of all her substance."

Sabrina groaned. "I've got to get myself a magazine rack," she said.

* * *

She also patched things up with Roxie and Josh.

That evening, she sat in her Aunts' kitchen, working on her laptop.

"I'm back to getting flooded with annoying e-mails," she muttered. "But from now on I'm not going to respond."

behaviour yesterday," Sabrina told everyone at the *Boston Citizen* the following day. "I had this really weird virus, which, for some reason, made me act like a total airhead."

Everyone stared at her. "I take my job seriously," Sabrina continued. "And I really appreciate the opportunity to be around professionals like you, even if it's just to make your coffee."

There was a silence. Sabrina's heart thumped with nervousness. Then Mike nodded.

"Well spoken. If you can write as well as you apologise, there's hope for you yet."

Sabrina still had her job!

"I have an idea," she said, when they started discussing what should go in the next edition.

"I don't know how you can top 'Guys and Thighs'" giggled one of the reporters.

But Sabrina had something better. One of the things she had been re-taught by her Aunts and me.

"It's something that's been on my mind," she told the group. "The three branches of government: is our system of checks and balances really working?"

"I love it," said Mike.

Sabrina beamed. Finally she had come up with something Mike liked.

"And I'm sure if 'U.S. News' hadn't just done the story," Mike finished. "Yours would have been much better."

"Good idea," nodded Zelda. "One never knows when there's an evil twin on the other end."

That was one thing we mortals never had to worry about!

"On the other hand," said Hilda, pointing. A delicious dish of pudding appeared. "They can't make pudding on command."

Sabrina grinned, hitting the 'send' button on her laptop.

"And they can't use magic to teach their evil twins a lesson. I just sent Katrina a 'Kill them with Kindness' spell."

In the Other Realm prison cell, Katrina suddenly found the urge to give Jezebelda a pedicure.

"Jezebelda," she panted like a faithful dog. "You're the smart one. You're the beautiful one."

"You are too kind," purred Jezebelda, enjoying every minute.

"I know," said Katrina through gritted teeth. "I'll get you for this, Sabrina!"

Spell Check!

That rotten witch Katrina has put another spell on my laptop. She's turned all my pictures into silhouettes! Can you match the pairs up, and find the odd one out?

Having a Blast!

Salem has been following clues to a treasure chest hidden inside this maze! Can you help him choose the right path? But beware – only one path leads to the treasure. The others lead… to his doom! *KAA-BOOM!*

Time After Time

Original story written by Dan Berendsen.

If you've ever broken up with a guy, you know how painful it can be. When Aunt Zelda broke up with her boyfriend, Professor Carlin from my college, she was devastated!

So much so, that she started cooking - her way of coping with heartache.

"That sounds like a very sensible way to deal with an emotional crisis," I told Aunt Hilda when I arrived at their house.

"Dinner is served," said Aunt Zelda, sliding open the door to the dining room.

I gaped at the sight of the dining room decked out like a Medieval feast. Torches were ablaze on the walls. A giant roast pig was in the centre of the table and food was piled up everywhere.

"The more upset she is, the bigger the spread," Salem explained, as he happily dove into the first course.

When I finally got to talk to Aunt Zelda alone, I discovered it wasn't actually Professor Carlin she was upset about losing. It was a guy she had walked away from, many years ago.

"Gabriel was a poet," she explained, opening up her heart. "A free-spirited witch who asked me to run away with him, get married, climb the Himalayas, and travel the galaxy. But like a fool I said no and sent him on his merry way."

"Why?" I asked. "He sounds perfect".

Aunt Zelda had decided her career and research were more important than love.

"Saying "no" to Gabriel is the biggest regret of my life," she sighed, wiping back the tears.

She showed me a picture of the two of them together taken at some hip, 1950's beatnik cafe.

"Wow. He's like a total babe," I said. "I can't believe you let this gorgeous hunk get away."

Oops! Bursting into tears again, Aunt Zelda ran up the stairs.

> "Wow. he's like a total babe," I can't believe you let this gorgeous hunk get away."

"Okay," I told myself. "I can definitely cross therapist off my list of career options."

So then, I had this crazy idea. If I could just go back in time and convince her to say "yes" to Gabriel's proposal, all her problems would be solved. Easy, right?

Inserting my magic CD-ROM into my laptop, I visited an Other Realm internet time travel company called Visitthepast.com. A techno-geek spokesman appeared on screen and told me to scan the picture of Aunt Zelda and Gabriel into the computer.

"I want to go back to the moment this picture was taken," I said.

There was a magical flash, and I disappeared into the computer screen…!

Moments later… I appeared in Greenwich Village in 1955, outside a sidewalk café.

There was Aunt Zelda and Gabriel, dressed like beatniks. Gabriel was tapping bongos and reciting some really awful poems. When he was done, he turned on the charm.

"Zelda," said Gabriel, stroking her hair. "There's something I have to ask you. Will you marry me?"

And this time, just as Aunt Zelda was about to turn him down, in stepped Yours Truly, who reminded her that nothing is more important than marrying your soulmate.

Of course, she didn't recognise me as her niece – who she'd never met, because I hadn't been born yet! - but she did listen to what I was saying, and…

"Yes, Gabriel. I will marry you," she said.

BINGO! Or should that be, Bongos?!

* * *

In a flash, I popped back out of my laptop and in to the present. It felt good to back in my room. Heck, it felt good to be back in the 21st century.

"That went well," I thought happily, heading for the kitchen in the off-campus house I shared with three friends. Apparently, time travel makes you hungry. I was rummaging through the fridge when Roxie and Morgan appeared.

"Excuse me, who are you?" demanded Morgan, glaring at me.

"And why are your grubby hands all over my string cheese?" asked Roxie, noticing the package of cheese I was holding.

The commotion roused Miles from his room.

"Who's the chick, and how come she's allowed to touch your cheese?" he asked Roxie.

Okay, something was very wrong here.

"Wait a minute," I said, alarm bells sounding in my head. "None of you know who I am?" They stared at me, shaking their heads.

"Then I should probably check

a few things on my computer," I said, bolting towards my room.

But when I opened the door my computer had gone – and so had all my other stuff!

Slamming the door, I pondered what to do, as my friends pounded to be let in.

"We're busting this door in three. Two. One." yelled Roxie.

Uh oh. I pointed at myself and disappeared…!

Heading back to my Aunts house, I planned to grab my magic book and sort out this mess. But my key wouldn't fit the lock of the front door.

Luckily, Aunt Zelda heard me and let me in. The house looked different somehow. One obvious change was the fact that the piano was gone.

"Just came by to say "hi" and grab a couple of things out of my old room," I explained to her. "Where's the piano?"

Aunt Zelda frowned. "We've never had a piano, and you don't have a room here, old or otherwise."

Okay, this was house number two I'd never lived in. Creepy!

Just then, Gabriel walked out of the dining room. I

could see some of his friends sitting around, talking poetry. So, he and Aunt Zelda were still happily married - that was something, anyway.

"You live with Hilda," Aunt Zelda was saying. "And Salem." Right.

"Well, I guess I'll leave you two to your domestic bliss and get back to my place," I laughed nervously, pointing at myself. "Hey, you wouldn't happen to know the address, would you?"

If you think that went badly, it was nothing compared to what happened when I arrived at Aunt Hilda's run-down, cramped, shabby apartment. She was now a terrible ventriloquist and Salem acted as her dummy! Trouble was, she kept moving her lips when he was talking!

"What's going on?!" I shouted, as the room rumbled from a train passing by the window. "Why are we living in a dump? I'm supposed to be in college!"

"Yeah, right," snorted Aunt Hilda. "Between your grades and what a ventriloquist brings home...I don't think so."

Confessing to my tinkering with the past didn't go down too well with Aunt Hilda, especially when she learned that she used to be happy, owned a successful business and was dating the president of a university.

"I'm sure I can fix it," I said, as she looked set to throttle me. "I just need to get back to that website. Where's your computer?"

"I sent it out to be detailed with my Rolls Royce," said Aunt Hilda, sarcastically.

I knew one place I for sure I could find a computer, so I headed for the offices of the *Boston Citizen*. I ran into my friend, Josh. You know, great the guy who had gotten me the internship there? But

he knew me only as a chicken delivery girl – and a bad one, at that!

"So, I guess the lesson here is," I groaned. "In the future, I'll never change the past!"

Things went from really bad to even worse when I discovered the time travel website had gone out of business.

"Let me guess," I said to the techno-geek spokesman. "Changing the past destroyed all your customers' lives?"

"Yeah, that's pretty much it," he agreed. Now what was I going to do? There had to be a way of getting my old life back.

Just then, Harvey turned up. Boy, was I happy to see him! Or, at least I thought I was.

"Your behaviour is totally unacceptable," he snapped. "When I agreed to hire you at the Chicken Shack, you and your probation officer promised me you'd clean up your act."

"I'm on probation?" I gagged. "And you're the manager at the Chicken Shack?"

Actually, he was only assistant manager, but he was still my boss.

That gave me an idea. "If you know me and Josh knows me," I said, hopefully. "Maybe I can just recreate my old life and it'll be like nothing ever happened."

Harvey glared at me. "I don't care what you do. "As long as you do it in the Chicken Mobile."

Chicken Mobile? Okay, I had to fix this. And fast!

I found Aunt Hilda and Salem in a cocktail lounge, performing their act. It was as pitiful as our lives. Aunt Hilda figured the only person who could possibly fix things was Aunt Zelda.

"And she and I don't really speak. We haven't got along since the day she and that poet – yeah, right! - got married," Aunt Hilda huffed.

"We can't ask her to give up her happiness for us," I argued. "There's got to be a way for Aunt Zelda to keep her happy life and for us to get ours back. If only I could get my hands on a magic book."

"Zelda's got tons of them," Aunt Hilda said. "We'll go as soon as we finish our next set."

"Go now!" shouted a customer.

"We'll go now," said Aunt Hilda.

Arriving at Aunt Zelda's house, we could hear loud arguing coming from inside. It was Aunt Zelda and Gabriel. Gabriel was telling her not to be rude to his guests.

"Guests?" she shrieked. "Don't you mean leeches? I am sick and tired of waiting on you and your pathetic posse of parasitic poets."

Ooh. Trouble in paradise.

Then they got to the real problem. It seems poetry's not very profitable.

"It always comes down to money," he complained.

"It does when one of us has to work three jobs to support us," countered Aunt Zelda. You promised to show me the galaxy. The closest I've come is your Ford Galaxy, and even then you brought your stupid friends."

"What are you saying?" demanded Gabriel. "You regret marrying me?"

"Every single day of my life."

That was music to my ears.

Gabriel stormed off and then Aunt Zelda spotted us on the porch. "I actually know how to get you out of your horrible marriage. Which is kind of my fault to begin with," I explained.

> "I don't know what you're talking about," she said, putting on a pretend smile. "Gabriel and I couldn't be happier.'

"With your clothes on?" asked Salem, sarcastically.

"Oh," said Aunt Hilda.

It didn't matter. Aunt Hilda and Salem's ventriloquist act kept them in stunned silence, allowing me to find the right spell in Aunt Zelda's magic book.

Reading the incantation out loud, I was transported back to Greenwich Village of 1955 again, and this time when Gabriel asked Aunt Zelda to marry him, I told her what she could expect.

"He's a user," I said. "He'll never live up to any of his promises. Your life and everyone else's life will be miserable."

"I was going to say "no" anyway," said Aunt Zelda. "But thanks for the support, whoever you are."

And that was finally that!

I returned to my Aunts' house in the present and everything and everyone was back to normal.

"Aunt Zelda," I said. "I know you're upset about Professor Carlin, but I just want you to know that you definitely made the right decision about Gabriel."

"I'm sure I did," she said.

What?? I thought she had regrets about not marrying him?

"Oh, please," she laughed. "I think about Gabriel every time a relationship ends. But then I remember the bad poetry, the hangers-on, and the fact that he always 'forgot' his wallet. Thank God I didn't end up with that deadbeat."

I groaned. "You couldn't have told me all this yesterday?"

Aunt Zelda smiled. "You didn't ask."

"I don't know what you're talking about," she said, putting on a pretend smile. "Gabriel and I couldn't be happier."

She was so clearly in denial.

"Do you know where she keeps her magic books?" I whispered to Aunt Hilda when Aunt Zelda went back to her 'guests'.

"In the front hall."

"Can you distract a room full of poets?" I asked.

"Easy," said Aunt Hilda.

Time Out!

How do you like this great Sabrina clock? Cool, eh? By telling the times listed below, discover six words to do with Sabrina's time travel adventure!

A Twenty past ten

B Quarter to twelve

C Twenty five to one

D Half past two

E Twenty five past eight

F Five to three

ANSWERS: A – Poetry, B – Ventriloquist, C – Marriage, D – Gabriel, E – Website, F – Soulmate

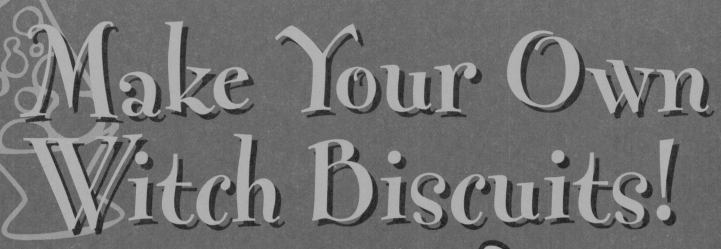

Make Your Own Witch Biscuits!

Sabrina tells me time travelling makes her really hungry, so I've made her some special gingerbread biscuits to take on her next trip. (Although, with the trouble she caused this time, I hope it's not soon!)

Why don't you make some to share with your friends? Make sure you ask an adult to help!

Gingerbread Stencils

Trace these stencils onto thin cardboard and carefully cut out with blunt-ended scissors. You will use these stencils to cut the dough before baking.

You will need

350g plain flour

5ml (teaspoon) of bicarbonate of soda

10ml (2 teaspoons) ground ginger

100g butter

175g soft brown sugar

60ml (4 tablespoons) golden syrup

1 egg, beaten

coloured soft icing and coloured icing pens (both obtainable from supermarkets)

1. Sift the flour, bicarbonate of soda and ginger into a mixing bowl. Rub in the butter until the mixture resembles fine bread crumbs, then stir in the sugar.

2. Beat the syrup into the egg then stir in the flour mixture. Mix together to make a smooth dough.

3. Knead the dough until smooth then divide in half. Roll out one half at a time on a floured surface until approximately 0.5cm thick.

4. Using your stencils, cut out until all the dough is used, re-rolling the trimmings. Repeat with the second half of the dough. Place on a greased baking tray.

5. Bake at 190 C (375 F) gas mark 5 for 12-15 minutes, until golden brown. Leave to cool slightly then carefully place your biscuits on a wire cooling tray until cold. Use the icing and icing pens to make faces on your biscuits.

Once your biscuits are ready – enjoy!

Time after Time!

Do you want to surprise your friends by guessing the number they're thinking, time after time? It's easy!

A	B	C	D
1	2	4	8
7	6	13	10
5	3	15	14
3	15	7	13
11	7	6	15
9	10	5	12
13	14	12	11
15	11	14	9

Ask a friend to think of a number between 1 and 15, but not to tell you. Without pointing it out, ask them which columns their number is in. Simply add the numbers at the very top of the columns, and you'll know the answer! For example, if they say their number is in columns C and D, add up the 4 and the 8 and you'll get 12. It works every time!

The Whole Ball of Wax

Original story written
by Laurie Gelman

You probably already know that my dad is a warlock, and my mom, who's name is Diana, is a human. Well, that's one of those things that annoys the Witches' Council, so they made one of their ridiculous, yet effective proclamations

And that proclamation was why I moved in with my aunts, Zelda and Hilda, when I turned 16 and got my powers. Since then, mom has spent most of her time in Peru on archaeological digs. We can keep in touch by letter, phone and e-mail, but the Witches' Council said if we ever meet face-to-face that rotten decree will kick in. So, we've played by their rules.

Well, except for that one day a few months ago…

The day began like any other… not that any day can be considered normal with the friends I have.

The house I share with Roxie, Miles and Morgan was overrun with long-legged fashion models.

"It's for my fashion design class," Morgan explained. "The final is going to be a spectacular fashion show featuring the students' creations. Designers from all over the world will be there."

Wow. I really hoped Morgan did well. She deserved it.

Miles, tongue almost hanging out, watched the models as Morgan led them upstairs.

"Boy," he sighed. "I'll bet any girl would kill to look like that."

I mean, please! "What do they have that I don't?" I asked him.

"Ten feet of legs," said Miles, exiting the room.

I thought about that for a second. "Hmm, I wouldn't mind ten feet of legs."

So I pointed to my legs, and Ping!, they stretched up ten feet – and I smashed my head on the ceiling!

"If I didn't have an eight foot ceiling," I groaned. Ouch.

* * *

The following morning, we all met at Aunt Hilda's Coffee House before class.

Miles had persuaded Morgan to let him film her models for a 'documentary' he was making (yeah, right!). Aunt Hilda thought they were too skinny so she told them she was serving fat-free lattes. (Actually, they were just normal lattes – expresso, whole milk and whipping cream!)

"Trust me," she told them. "These are going to taste just like the real thing."

Morgan took a sip. "If I didn't know better, I'd say that was real whipped cream," she said.

Aunt Hilda passed around a plate. "And here's what I say – Who's up for fat-free, chocolate cheesecake?"

All three models raised their hands!

Later that morning, I had this weird feeling that I was being spied on. In fact, I'd had the feeling for a few days. I kept seeing a shadowy figure following me, and then disappearing again. It was downright creepy!

Well, when I saw the mystery person in the college hallways, ducking and diving every time I turned around, I'd had enough.

I led them on a merry chase through the classrooms, until I came to the chemistry lab. Grabbing a beaker, I waited for them to follow. I didn't have to wait long.

"Okay, the jig is up..." I said, then stared in disbelief at the attractive woman before me.

"Mom?!" I gasped, dropping the beaker in shock.

The woman smiled.

"Yes, sweetheart. It's me."

I couldn't believe it! "What are you doing here?"

My mom stared down at the broken beaker on the floor. "Well, originally, I just came to see you," she said. "Now I guess I'll be sweeping up glass."

Then I remembered the decree of the Witches' Council.

"The Witches' Council said if we ever came face-to-face, you'd be turned into a ball of wax," I told her.

Mom knew this, but every year she had been flying up from Peru to check up on me without me knowing.

"But this year, you changed the game plan," she said.

Then it struck me. We were looking at each other, and she wasn't a ball of wax!

"I guess the Witches' Council decided to nullify the decree," she said, as we gave each other a big, loving hug.

It was then that she changed into a wax blob the size of a bowling ball.

"So much for that theory," I groaned.

I gathered up "mom" and rushed straight to my Aunts house.

"The Witches' Council is a bunch of evil, passive-aggressive control freaks," growled Aunt

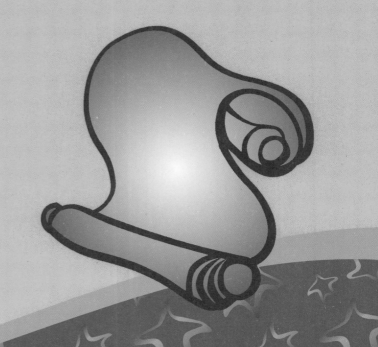

Zelda, when I explained what had happened. "Although I must say, that Burt Schlegel is a doll."

"Could he help us get Mom back to her pre-paraffin self?" I asked, watching Aunt Hilda feed Mom the bowling ball some raisin cake.

"No harm in going over there and asking," said Aunt Zelda. Even Salem liked the idea.

"While we're there," he purred. "Maybe the Witches' Council will find it in their hearts to show me some mercy."

I glared at him. "Innocent mother desperate to see her daughter, fascist cat who tried to take over the world…yeah, you've got a shot."

Trouble was, neither did my mom!

The old Witches' Council run by Burt Schlegel was no longer around. They had been considered too old and put out to pasture. Literally.

"Awful…" groaned Aunt Zelda. "The thought of that elegant Burt Schlegel nibbling on grass."

The new Witches' Council was three Yuppie twenty-somethings who were more interested in trying to set up a date with Hercules and worrying about lunch appointments.

"All right. We've heard your pitch," said the chief council member after I'd pleaded for mom to be returned to normal. "We can't undo the old decree, but there are a few other options. We can turn your mom into a throw pillow, a mohair scarf, or a glass eye. Your choice."

"Honey," said mom, tucked under my arm. "If it's all the same to you, I'll stay wax."

I was devastated!

"Don't worry, mom," I told her, giving her a hug. "We'll get you out of this. In the meantime, I'm going to find you the most beautiful wax ball

stand money can buy!"

Oooh! I was furious with that stupid Witches' Council! How dare they do this to my mom?!!

Aunt Zelda promised to traipse around every pasture in the Other Realm until she found Burt Schlegel. Perhaps he had the answers.

"And what is mom supposed to do in the meantime," I snapped sarcastically. "Wax down a few surfboards?"

What we did, was spend some quality time together. (As much quality time as you can have with a wax ball!!)

We went to the coffee house, had our pictures taken in a photo booth, took a ride on a tandem, and then I showed her around the newspaper office where I worked.

"Honey, I'm so proud of you," she said.

My heart was breaking. "Thanks. Your support really means a lot to me."

After that, I took mom back to my house, where madness was in full swing, as usual.

Morgan was panicking about the fashion show, not helped by Miles following her and the models around everywhere with a camcorder. Clothes and accessories were strewn everywhere.

"Miles, I can't iron with that lens in my face," she yelled, busy steam ironing a shirt for one of her male models.

"Sorry," he said. "I have a cinematic duty to capture every second of your complete emotional breakdown."

She threw a leather miniskirt at him.

"Good," he encouraged her, still filming. "More of that."

The girl models were struggling to fit into their outfits. They couldn't understand how they'd gained weight.

"All I've had for a week are Hilda's fat-free lattes and muffins," moaned one.

This was too much for Morgan. She blew up at everyone. The

models, in turn, walked out on her!

"What have I done?" she groaned. "This show means everything to me. Designing clothes is the only thing I have a real talent for, except for curling my eyelashes in a moving car. But I can't make a living doing that."

"Come on!" I said, putting mom down on the counter, a little too close to the steam iron, before hurrying out of the house with Morgan. "Maybe we can get them back."

Mom started to sweat from the steam coming from the iron.

"Is it hot in here," she called out to an empty house. "Or is it just me?"

When I got back I walked into – nightmare city! Mom had completely melted all over the counter!

"Omigod! This is

> With techno-music blaring out we gave it our all. The audience went wild!

Morgan out now that she had lost all her models, I persuaded my friends to walk down the fashion runway.

The trouble was, we were no supermodels! The night of the fashion show, we took turns

horrible!" I screamed.

I rushed over, trying to moosh the melted wax back into a ball. It was hopeless.

"Look at you," I sobbed, tears running down my face. "What have I done? We were just getting to know each other. Now I've lost you forever. Mom, I'm so sorry!"

I cried and I cried…

And my tears began falling onto the melted wax. WHOOSH! The wax turned back into mom! My real, human mom.

"Mom!" I gasped. "How did…?"

Aunt Zelda and Aunt Hilda appeared out of nowhere. Aunt Hilda was holding a magic book.

"Sabrina, great news," she said. "I just found out if you melt wax and mix it with your tears…" She stared at mom. "Oh, you figured it out. But there's one other thing… don't look at each other!"

Mom was mom again, but if we looked at each other ever again, she'd turn into another ball of wax and remain that way… forever!

Heartbreaking as it was, we had to say goodbye.

"Don't cry, darling," she said, as we turned our backs on each other and I started sobbing again. "We'll do what we've always done… write… call…"

"And who knows," said Aunt Hilda, trying to make me feel better. "With the turnover rate on the Witches' Council, pretty soon we can appeal to a whole new group of idiots."

Mom and I each put a hand behind our back. We held each other tightly.

"I love you, mom," I sobbed.

"I love you, too," said mom.

Sometimes, life can be tough…

To take my mind off losing my mom again, and to help

walking down the catwalk in front of an audience of famous fashion designers.

Talk about nerves!

Morgan, Roxie and I showed off the women's outfits, Josh, Harvey and Miles the men's.

Well, stumbled, tripped and fell down the catwalk would be a better description!

"This is a disaster," groaned Morgan backstage, after we'd all embarrassed her at least once. "I'm ruined!"

I grabbed a beautiful dress from the rails. "Hold on. We still have evening wear. And I've a feeling things will go a lot better this time."

Without anyone noticing, I pointed my finger…!

Suddenly, my friends and I were the most confident supermodels to hit the catwalks.

With techno-music blaring out, and under the glare of strobe lights, we gave it our all. The audience went wild! They rose up and started chanting "Morgan!", "Morgan!". She was soon lost in a sea of journalists!

"You were great, sweetheart," Aunt Zelda told me, as we stood on the catwalk after the show. "But technically, you shouldn't have used your pointing finger to make Morgan look good."

I shrugged. "I know. But Morgan's really talented, and I wanted people to see that."

Aunt Hilda laughed. "Ooh, good one. Way to find the loophole."

I sighed. It would have been great if mom could have been there to see me.

And then I noticed a shadowy figure leaving the auditorium. It was mom. Keeping her back turned, she waved to me.

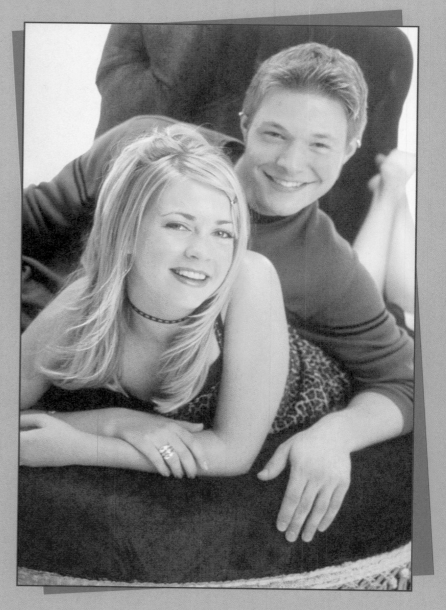

I smiled and waved back.

The next morning, we all met up at the coffee house.

Morgan read us her rave reviews in all the newspapers!

"I'm behind you one hundred percent," said Aunt Hilda. "And just to show my support, I've made you a couple of my fat-free double chocolate cream pies."

She put a couple of delicious-looking pies in front of Morgan, who took a spoonful.

"I don't know how you do it," she said, licking her lips.

"Try getting into those slacks in two weeks," said Aunt Hilda, grinning. "And you'll know!"

Sabrina
The Teenage
Witch

Morgan's

Thanks to my friend's help, the fashion show went much better than I ever expected! Here are two more of my designs, but I really need your help to choose the colour schemes. Colour in

Fashion Show

the dresses for me...
let your imagination run
wild! You could also glue
glitter onto the designs –
but remember not to shut
the book until the glue is
completely dry!

Use these examples for
ideas, but go mad with
your own designs!

A Superstitious Lot!

I always thought the Witches' Council's spell on my mom was just a silly superstition… unfortunately, it turned out it wasn't, after all!

Here are some of my favourite superstitions from around the world, because lots of people are superstitious - both witches and humans! (And even some cats – Salem)

Left-handed people in India are considered a bad omen, and are chased out of town! (If that includes left-pawed cats, it's a good thing I'm quick! – Salem)

If you bite your tongue while eating, it's because you've recently told a lie. This is where the saying 'bite your tongue' comes from.

The devil can enter your body when you sneeze. Having someone say, "God bless you" drives the devil away.

The number of Xs on your hand is the number of children you'll have.

The Chinese believe that you will go broke if you use scissors on New Year's Day.

Seeing an ambulance is very unlucky unless you pinch your nose, touch your toes or hold your breath until you see a black or brown dog! (For some of us, seeing the dog is worse luck! – Salem)

In Afghanistan, if you don't cover your bald head, it will start raining.

82

It's unlucky for a cat to sneeze in your house. (Too bad. I'm not going out in the cold when I'm sick! – Salem)

Golfers will have a successful day on the course if they start their round with odd-numbered clubs, and don't use a ball numbered higher than four. Tiger Woods always wears something red on Sundays for good luck!

If an eyelash falls out, put it on the back of your hand, make a wish and throw it over your shoulder. If it flies off the hand, your wish will come true.

An acorn on the windowsill will keep lightning out!

If a black cat walks towards you, it brings good fortune, but if it walks away, it takes good luck with it. (No comment. – Salem)

In Roman times, people used to look at their reflections in the water, believing them to be glimpses of the soul. Any disruption to the water would bring bad luck to the person looking in. This superstition continues today with the fear of seven years bad luck for breaking a mirror!

If your right ear starts itching, someone speaks well of you. If your left ear twitches, someone speaks ill of you. (If both ears twitch, check for fleas – Salem)

A swarm of bees settling on the roof of a house, means that the house will burn down! (Sure, if you set fire to the beehive! – Salem)

In Africa, if you shave your head on a Saturday, you'll always be in debt!

Rain is highly likely when a cat busily washes it's ears! (Hey, no fair looking! I don't watch you in the tub, do I? – Salem)

If you pat a pig, you'll get stomach ache! (If you eat a pig you'll get a stomach ache too. Trust me. Stop after the first couple of sausages. Me-ooow. – Salem)

Sabrina's Book Bag

I'm always carrying loads of books to college, so Morgan designed me this fashionable book bag. Here's how you can make your own…! Ask a grown-up to help you. Even though I'm pretty much a grown-up, I'd still need Morgan to help me!

1. Take a piece of fur fabric and cut to the size of 60cm x 30cm. Trim one long edge by folding over approximately 10mm and sewing full length.

2. Fold fabric face together and sew one side and the bottom. (Do not sew neatened edge.) Turn right side out. To make handles, you'll need 45cm x 25m of webbing ribbon or decorative rope (you can get this at craft shops).

3. Sew these on to the bag in position show. (See below.) Decorate the bag to your own design.

If made from towelling material, you could use it as a beach bag, decorated with stencil cut-outs of fish, star fish, bucket and spade, etc.!

Dressing Up!

The girls are going for a night on the town! Follow the lines to see what dresses they'll be wearing!

ANSWERS: A – Aunt Hilda, B – Morgan, C – Roxie, D – Sabrina

"I, Busybody"

Original story written by Adam England

Ever heard the story about the girl who fell for a cat? No? Well, let me tell you…the girl in question was my roommate Roxie, the cat…Salem, who else?

It happened when Salem phoned an Indian restaurant to order dinner. He accidentally called my house instead

"Sorry, dude, wrong number," said Roxie, answering the phone. "You must've mis-programmed your speed dial… hey, how did you know my name was Roxie…?"

Salem covered his mistake by praising Roxie for her radio show. She fell for it hook, line and sinker.

"He's actually kind of cool," she told me, when I asked five minutes later why she was still talking to a wrong number.

Not realising who it was, I encouraged her to keep talking. She never knew it could be Mr. Right.

"Good thinking. Thanks Sabrina."

"I'm here to help," I said.

I was also helping Harvey. Morgan had just blown up at him for not getting her an invite to a private party.

"You shouldn't let Morgan push you around like that," I told him, after she had stormed out.

"Every time you do what she wants, she

loses respect for you. You have to stand up to her."

"You're right," he agreed. "Thanks, Sabrina."

"I'm here to help," I said.

Roxie was still talking to Salem.

"Since you already know who I am, why don't you tell me about yourself?" she asked. "Start with your name."

"My name," said Salem, trying to sound like a real hunk. "Is...Alejandro."

Oh, brother!

I kept helping people even when I went to work at Aunt Hilda's Coffee House.

She was thinking of buying Aunt Zelda a sweater for her birthday.

"She'll hate it," I said.

"Sabrina, I've lived with the woman for 650 years," Aunt Hilda reminded me. "I think I know my sister."

"Then you know her birthday was last week," I said.

I suggested that she use Aunt Zelda's broken antique tea set to make a mosaic table top or planter – she'd love it.

"Great," said Aunt Hilda. "Thanks, Sabrina."

"I'm here to help," I said.

I also helped Miles, with a speeding ticket. I told him to contest it in court. The State Troopers who wrote the tickets never showed up for the trial, so the judge would throw out the ticket.

Next it was Mike, my editor at the *Boston Citizen* newspaper. He stopped in for coffee and was in an even worse mood than usual. The owners of the paper were refusing to give him a raise, even though he had given them twenty years of dedicated service.

I told him to fight for it. Demand more money!

"You've got a point," he said. "I'm going down to HQ to give them a piece of my mind."

"I'm here to help," I said, beaming. Then I called out to the whole coffee house. "All right, who else needs help? I'm on a roll. Give me somebody."

A few days later, I caught up with Miles at after his day in court.

He had followed my advice, but the State Trooper had shown up after all. Miles got fined, and then got fined again when the same State Trooper pulled him over on his way home because of a broken tail light.

"Another fifty bucks," he growled. "Thanks, Sabrina."

"I was only trying to help," I called out as he stomped off.

Aunt Zelda had hated Aunt Hilda's gift. She had covered Aunt Zelda's briefcase with a mosaic of broken china.

"Where did she get such a numbskull idea?" Aunt Zelda demanded when I saw her. "I would have been happy with a sweater."

Oh, well...

And when Mike took my advice he ended up with a pay cut and the loss of his health benefits!

Harvey had pretty bad results too. Standing up to Morgan resulted in her telling him she didn't want to be friends anymore.

"Every language has a word for people like you," he muttered when I ran into him on the porch of my house.

I groaned. "I know. In English, it's 'busybody'."

"That would be the cleaned-up version," he growled.

That did it. I went into the house and looked up the Other Realm Yellow Pages on my laptop.

"'Buddy's Busy Body Shop'" I read, after searching for awhile.

Bingo! I pointed

myself into the computer.

The Busy Body Shop was a typical greasy garage. I told the owner, Buddy, that I was and out-of-control busybody. He said it was a common problem. All he'd need to do was tweak a part called my gyro.

Forget tweaking – I got Buddy to take it out. I would never interfere again...!

* * *

Meanwhile, Aunt Hilda had discovered that Salem was having a phone fling with Roxie.

"There will be no inter-species dating under my roof," she told him, sternly. "What do you think Roxie's going to do when she finds out that Mr. Right has a tail?"

When I arrived back at the coffee shop, Aunt Hilda filled me in on everything including the fact that Salem and Roxie had set up a date!

"What your cat and my best friend choose to do with their free time is absolutely none of my business," I said.

Wow. Having the busybody gyro removed really was working.

I spotted Harvey, glaring at Morgan. She was wrapped around some older guy who's wife turned out to be the number one female kickboxer of the state. And the jealous type.

"I'm worried about Morgan even though I hate her right now," he said, hoping I'd interfere. But when I went over to her table I just gave them a re-fill. Hey, I'm no busybody!

Later, when I got to the newspaper office, Mike was on the warpath. No one could find the pictures Josh took of some strange cloud formation the night before.

He claimed he gave the pictures to Jerry, the photo editor, but Jerry said he didn't. Mike took Jerry's side and assumed Josh was lying to protect himself.

"We were standing right over there," said Josh defensively. "Sabrina was with me." He looked pleadingly at me. "You saw me hand Jerry the disk. Tell them."

I had seen Josh hand over the disk, but because I'd had my gyro removed, it was no longer possible for me to interfere. So I simply said, "This really isn't any of my business."

Mike went ballistic, and threatened to fire Josh if he ever lied again. Then he stormed off.

"Thanks a lot, Sabrina," snapped Josh.

"No problem," I said, smiling happily. "I'm not here to help."

Then Josh got really mad. "Sabrina, I needed

> "So I haven't been a perfect cat, but I'm willing to change for Roxie.
> I'm in love with her."

Sabrina the Teenage Witch

> ## "Just a momentary seizure of elation caused by your rapturous beauty…"

your help and you bailed on me. And now my job is hanging by a thread."

"I didn't mean to put your job in jeopardy," I said defensively.

"Then why did you?" Josh demanded.

"I don't know. Why did I let Morgan seduce a married kickboxer? Why am I letting Roxie date a cat?"

"What do you mean Roxie's dating a cat? Have you completely lost it?"

"Yeah," I groaned. "And I think I'd better go get it back."

Unfortunately, Buddy had already sold my busy body gyro to someone. Luckily, he kept generic replacements in his shop. In no time Buddy had installed a brand new busybody part inside of me. I was good to go…or not…

I owned up to Mike that I saw Josh hand the pictures to Jerry… and then went on to criticise Mike's house and choice of neckwear.

Oh great. I'd gone from being a busybody to being an obnoxious busybody!

While all this was happening, Salem was pleading with Aunt Zelda to turn him back into a man so he could date Roxie. But she reminded him that the Witches' Council had rules against that.

"I curse the Witches' Council!" hissed Salem. "Unless they're listening," he recoiled. "So I haven't been a perfect cat, but I'm willing to change for Roxie. I'm in love with her." Aunt Zelda watched in astonishment as Salem began to cry.

"Are those tears?" she gasped. "This is the real thing."

"That's what I'm trying to tell you," sniffed Salem.

Aunt Zelda agreed to request a temporary transformation from the Witches' Council so Salem could meet Roxie in human form.

"But I'm warning you," she

said, sternly. "Unless she really is the one, the spell won't last."

Salem was too overjoyed to listen. "I'm going to be a man," he sang. "I'm going to be a man. Omigosh! What am I going to wear?"

* * *

I got to 'Buddy's Busy Body Shop' just as he was writing a receipt for an incredibly gorgeous woman. I could only imagine what parts he'd replaced in her. I told Buddy my problem and he hooked me up to a diagnostic machine to find out why my body was rejecting the new busybody gyro.

It seemed that my original busybody part came with a 'compassion' upgrade.

"When you were getting involved in other people's business," he explained. "It was because you were sincerely trying to help."

"So I wasn't really a busybody. I was just concerned about my friends." Boy, was I relieved! "Well, Buddy, get started and build me a new one of those gizmos. What can I do to help?"

Buddy fired up a welder's torch.

"Try to hold still," he said.

* * *

A little while later, Salem kept his date with Roxie at Aunt Hilda's Coffee House. He was no longer a cat – but a good-looking man!

"Alejandro, I can't believe we're actually meeting," gasped Roxie "You're exactly as I pictured you."

"Who would have thought," said Salem. "A craving for chutney could lead to an inseparable bond between two…uh…"

Just then, Veronique, the dish I'd seen in Buddy's shop, walked across the room. Salem couldn't take his eyes off her.

"Alejandro?" said Roxie, puzzled.

"Thanks, Veronique," I said, staring at a guilt-ridden Salem.

"My pleasure, Sabrina," she said. "He made it too easy."

She pointed at herself and disappeared.

"I've been had! Duped!" moaned Salem, realising that I had set him up. "Actually, I was duped before I even got the chance to be had!"

With that out of the way, I went into the coffee house to make my apologies to my friends.

"The reason I get involved in your lives is because I care about you," I told them. "True, my advice doesn't work out so well on occasion. Okay. Quite often and not at all. But, if you ever need my help, don't hesitate to ask. I can't turn down a friend in need. It's just not the way I'm 'built'"

My grovelling did the trick. Harvey told me that by not having to take Morgan out to expensive places, he could focus on more important things. Like digging himself out of debt!

And Morgan had given up the kickboxer when she had found out he was married.

At the newspaper office, Jerry had found the missing disk with the cloud pictures and Mike and Josh straightened everything out between them.

When I got back to their house, I apologized to my aunts for butting into their lives as well.

"I just can't help it," I said.

"Of course you can't," agreed Aunt Hilda. "It's in the Spellman genes. Why else would I always be snooping through Zelda's purse and reading her diary?"

"Hilda!" gasped Aunt Zelda, shocked.

Aunt Hilda smiled. "It's because I care."

I smiled, too. And so did Aunt Zelda. Then, as we all raised our re-glued, re-assembled, still looking simply awful antique teacups, I said, proudly, "Caring is a good thing. It's one of the qualities that makes us unique. I propose a toast. To the caring, busybody Spellmans."

"Just a momentary seizure of elation caused by your rapturous beauty…" said Salem, quickly. Then Veronique walked by again. She gave Salem a wink.

"Me-ow!" purred Salem, excitedly.

Roxie saw the woman, too.

"I knew it," she snapped, turning her back on him. "You're just another pig."

Make that just another cat. Poof! Salem reverted to fur form, and he was dressed in a small suit.

"Dagnabbit!" he growled, escaping before anyone could see him.

I stopped him just as he ran out the door. Veronique met me outside as well. Seems my plan and my re-calibrated gyro both worked.

Witch Supplies!

You wouldn't believe the amount of supplies you need to be a witch! Can you put the following witch words into this grid? But be careful, one word doesn't fit, at all! Can you guess which one it is?

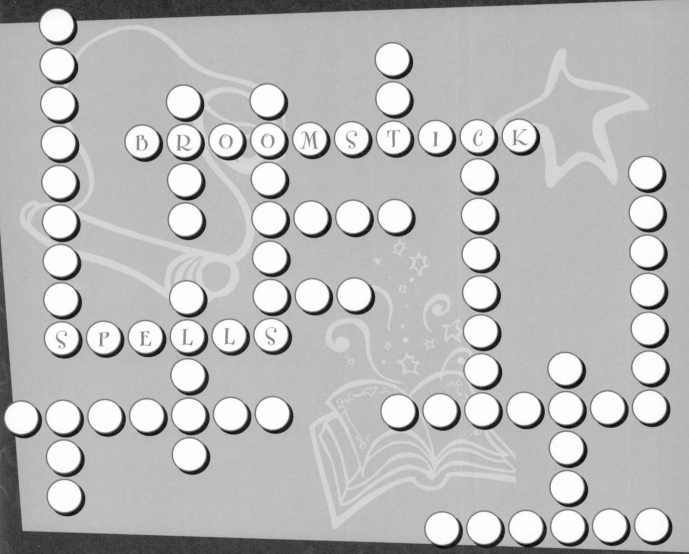

3 Letters
BAT, CAT, HAT

4 Letters
FROG, WAND

5 Letters
BLACK, CLOAK

6 Letters
CACKLE SPELLS

7 Letters
CANDLES, COBWEBS,
POTIONS, SCREAMS,
SPIDERS

8 Letters
CAULDRON

9 Letters
HOURGLASS

10 Letters
BROOMSTICK

I've got to learn to curb my interference in other people's business, even if I do it with the best intentions! But that started me wondering...are YOU a busybody?! Take my test and find out!

Are you

Question 1

Are you
a) A good listener
b) Someone who speaks first without thinking through the consequences
c) Too busy with your own life to worry about other people's problems!

Question 2

If a friend had a problem, would you
a) Wait for them to ask your advice
a) Tell them what they should do straight away
a) Tell them you've got problems of your own!

Question 3

A friend is in trouble at school. Do you
a) Tell them to tell the truth - it's better to be honest and admit their mistakes
b) Tell them to make up a lie - and hope they're not found out!
c) Make believe you don't know them until the problem passes

a Busybody?

Question 4

Are you the type of person who
a) Is sensitive of hurting people's feelings
b) If there's bad news you'll tell them whether or not it upsets them
c) People have feelings? Who knew?

Question 7

You have the chance of writing an advice column in your school newspaper. Do you
a) Politely decline the offer – you would hate to accidentally give bad advice to someone
b) Take the job at once! You always know best!
c) Advise the school to stop publishing a newspaper.

Question 5

Your friend decides she doesn't want a fuss on her birthday. Do you
a) Comply with her wishes - it's her day, and if that's what she wants, you respect her decision
a) Organise a wild party for her whether she wants one or not
c) Throw a party and tell everyone it's YOUR birthday

Question 8

Your friend is about to buy an outfit that you know will look awful on her. Would you
a) Show her another outfit that would suit her and tell her she'd look even better in this one
b) Tell her how awful she'd look and then proceed to choose an outfit for her.
c) Let her buy the outfit – it's her money.

Question 6

Your friend's Walkman has died Do you
a) Treat her to a new one
b) Take the old one apart to fix it because you always know what you're doing
c) Tell her get up to date with an MP3.

Mostly A's: You are a true friend! Never interfering, but always there if someone needs you!

Mostly B's: You're a good friend, but you are definitely a busybody! Try to keep your opinions to yourself!

Mostly C's: With your attitude, it's amazing you have any friends!

Perfume

I can't believe I'm getting married! I want to smell really good for the wedding, and thanks to Zelda, I won't have to buy anything expensive. She makes the best perfume around! Why not make yourself some nice-smelling perfume to wear or to give a friend as a present? It's easy! But still ask an adult for help, because science can be sloppy And, make sure to start "brewing your potion" far enough in advance of any special day, because this takes about four weeks from start to finish.

You will need

A small glass jar with a tight-fitting lid

Water

An assortment of fresh petals from a flower shop that are highly perfumed (Roses and carnations are best)

An empty perfume bottle

A perfume funnel (which you can buy at the chemists)

Ribbon to make a bow

1. Buy a bunch of freshly-cut flowers and take off all the petals. Make sure the glass jar is thoroughly clean and dry. One at a time, places the petals in the jar until it is completely full.

Power!

2. Fill the jar with water until it is completely full and can take no more. Screw the lid back on very tightly and shake the jar vigorously. Leave to settle for a few days.

3. Open the jar to see if the petals have soaked up any of the water. If so, fill to the brim with water again. Screw the lid back on very tightly and leave it for four weeks.

4. Strain and carefully pour the perfume through the funnel into the empty perfume bottle. Tie a ribbon around the bottle into a bow. And now you have your very own home made perfume to wear!

Eau de Fun

To Sabrina Love Aunt Hilda xxx

Sabrina's Secret Soulmate!

Wow! All this stuff about soulmates makes me wonder who mine will be! You might find the answer in this puzzle!

START →

Starting in the top left hand corner, follow the letters up, down, across or backwards and see how many men's names listed below you can find. Rearrange the leftover letters and they will spell someone's name you have already found. Is this going to be my soulmate? You never know!

The names to look for are:

PRESIDENT BANNING

JOSH   LUKE

SALEM SABERHAGEN

well, he *was* a man in his past life!)

WILL   MILES   HARVEY KINKLE

```
S A U E S O L K
L L E M H J E N
H R E S L E K I
A G B A V K Y E
N E K S I D E V
W I L E B T N R
I M E R A I N A
L L S P N N G H
```

ANSWERS: My soulmate might be ... Luke!

I Fall to Pieces!

Original story
written by
Jon Vandergriff

Boy, there seem to have been plenty of relationship break-ups in my life recently. First Aunt Zelda, then me and mom, and finally poor Aunt Hilda went through it. But for her, there was a happy ending…!

Not that she was feeling so happy to start with. President Banning from the university had just broken up with her, so she decided she was through with men.

Not only was she through with them, she was purposely ignoring all male customers in her coffee house!

"Aunt Hilda," I said, when I arrived for work. "I'm sorry about you and President Banning, but it's no reason to take it out on all men. There's a better way to deal with your feelings."

"I know, I know," she grumbled. "Talk through it. Feel the pain. I'd rather cause the pain."

"Or…" I suggested. "We could go shopping."

Aunt Hilda grabbed her bag. "I like your way," she said.

With Aunt Zelda in tow, headed to an outlet mall in the Other Realm.

"You were right about curing Hilda's break-up blues," Aunt Zelda said, as we wandered around a store called 'Potions, Lotions and Notions', watching Aunt Hilda grabbing things off shelves and shoving them in her basket. "Shopping is just what the doctor ordered."

"Yeah, but the doctor didn't order six hours of it," I grumbled. We told Aunt Hilda that we'd shopped 'til we dropped and would meet her back at her house. She didn't seem to mind at all.

"You two lallygaggers have been slowing me down," she proclaimed.

Meanwhile, Harvey was just arriving at my house for a game of poker with the gang.

Now Harvey is the worst poker player, ever! He's never won a game in all the years I've known him. Josh on the other hand is a master at cards. He wins all the time.

Thanks to Salem, all that was about to change.

He caught Harvey before he rang the bell, and made him a proposition.

"You're a guy who stinks at poker," Salem told him bluntly. "I'm a cat with no scruples. Here's the deal. During the game, I'll sit behind Josh and let you know what he's got. You'll be the winner, and we'll split the take 80-20."

Harvey was horrified. "Salem, that's cheating."

Salem snorted in contempt. But the cat can be persuasive, and Harvey WAS sick of losing to Josh, so he agreed...! Oh, Harvey! How could you?

Back at my Aunts house, Aunt Hilda finally returned, laden down with packages, including a huge gift box.

"What's in the box?" I asked. "A refrigerator? A washer-dryer combo?"

Aunt Hilda tore off the wrapping and opened the box. Out stepped a man, who proceeded to kiss Aunt Hilda!

"A fiancé," she said. I recognised the guy. It was Will, the conductor from the Halloween Mystery Train.

It seems they met when Aunt Hilda popped into 'Just Cauldrons' to check out the latest models, and the saleslady was showing Will the same cauldron Aunt Hilda had just been looking at. They fell immediately in love!

"Oh, and before I forget," she said, after finishing her story. "The wedding's this weekend."

Aunt Zelda and I grabbed her and hurried into the kitchen!

I tried to explain that she had just broken up with President Banning, and that she might be acting a little impulsively, because she was on the rebound.

"I'm telling you," said Aunt Hilda. "I know true love when I see it at the mall. And this is it. Now If you'll excuse me, Will and I have to go pick out our rings."

Great idea I had, taking her shopping! We couldn't let her get married to a guy she bonded with over cauldrons.

"I don't think we have a choice," Aunt Zelda told me. "The oddest part is that on the mystery train, I could have sworn Will fancied me."

That gave me an idea! I told Aunt Zelda that when they came back, I'd keep Aunt Hilda distracted in the kitchen, while she threw herself at Will.

He would succumb to her charms, and then we'd let Aunt Hilda catch him in a compromising position and she'd come to her senses.

Well, it seemed a good idea at the time!

Back at my house, Josh, Roxie, Morgan and Miles could not believe Harvey's sudden good luck with cards. He had won every game, and was scooping in piles and piles of money. Their money!

Miles was staring at Salem, who was seated on the windowsill behind Josh. "I swear Sabrina's cat is humming 'If I Were A Rich Man'!"

Of course, no one except a grinning Harvey believed him!

By the time Aunt Hilda and Will returned with their rings – mood rings! – Aunt Zelda

was dressed in her skimpiest red dress.

I ushered Aunt Hilda into the kitchen, pointing before I disappeared through the door. The lights lowered, and romantic jazz music started playing.

Aunt Zelda pinned Will down on the sofa and gave him a big kiss.

My cue to bring Aunt Hilda back out!

She was horrified by what she was seeing, and wouldn't believe Will when he told her Aunt Zelda tried to have her wicked way with him.

"You betrayed me!" she snapped angrily. She pointed, zapping him back to the mall.

"I'm so sorry, Aunt Hilda," I said, comforting her, trying not to smile. "But I guess this just proves he's not your true love, after all."

Aunt Hilda started to cry. Then she froze – literally! – and shattered into pieces!

"I can't believe it," Aunt Zelda gasped, looking down at a broken Aunt Hilda. "The only time a witch falls to pieces is when she's separated from her soulmate. We were wrong, Sabrina. They really were in love!"

I groaned. "And we got the bright idea to break them up."

"Actually, honey," said Aunt Zelda. "That was you."

Kick me when I'm down, why don't you?

I felt horrible. We had to bring Aunt Hilda back to life.

We tried gluing the shattered pieces together – it looked awful!

"This is a lot harder than Mr. Potato Head," I groaned.

Aunt Zelda weaved some magic and the famous French artist, Rodin,

Sabrina the Teenage Witch

> ## "I'm getting married next," she cheered. "Everybody start shopping. I need flatwear and a bagel slicer."

appeared. He sculpted a perfect Aunt Hilda, but even he couldn't bring her back to life.

"I am an artist, not a genetic engineer," he said, handing me a business card. "You've got to call a specialist."

The 'specialist' was Ed at 'Ed's Life and Storage Warehouse. We revive your loved ones at factory direct prices.' This was perfect, although Aunt Zelda didn't think so.

"I've heard about this quack," she said. "I'm not putting my sister's fate in his hands."

Unfortunately, we had no other choice.

I pointed. Aunt Hilda and I disappeared, reappearing in a creepy, cluttered warehouse, full of frozen witches covered in dust and cobwebs.

"Okay," I said, heart sinking. "I get the 'storage' part, but I'm not seeing a lot of life here."

Ed made rather a dramatic entrance which only enhanced the creep factor.

"In exchange for reviving your Aunt," he said, after I explained what I needed. "You must be willing to give up your true love. Are you willing to risk your own love life to save your Aunt's?"

Well, as much as I hated it, I was the one who had caused all this…so I agreed.

We shook hands. As we did, a glowing ball of energy travelled from my hand to Ed's. He touched Aunt Hilda, and the energy ball was transferred to her. She was enveloped in a sparkling glow… and came back to life!

"What a rush!" gasped Aunt Hilda.

Of course, I had to explain what had

happened. I told her how sorry I was.

"Not half as sorry as I am," said Aunt Hilda. "I've got to go find my true love. Again."

I returned to my house to find the poker game still going. Harvey had just won his twelfth game in a row.

Seeing Harvey wink at Salem, I knew immediately how he had gotten so lucky.

"I've got a feeling your luck's about to change," I muttered, pointing at Salem.

And it did. Every time Harvey asked out loud whether he should fold, Salem sneezed. So Harvey said out loud that perhaps he would stay in the game. Salem sneezed again. He sneezed so much, Harvey didn't know what he should do and lost the game – and all the money.

"Finally, all is right with the world," said Josh, scooping up the pot. "Kinkle's a loser again."

"The cat's not doing so good either," said Miles, as Salem sneezed uncontrollably. That would teach them to cheat!

Saturday arrived, and the wedding was on again.

Aunt Hilda was holding it in the back yard of the house, which had been beautifully, decorated with a flowered arch; and the whole garden was decked out in decorations and balloons.

One problem… Will, the minister and all the guests had been waiting for an hour and a half, and there was still no sign of Aunt Hilda.

I went to check and found her in her bedroom with Aunt Zelda. Both were hugging and crying.

"I'm going to miss all of you all so much," sobbed Aunt Hilda.

I tried to tell her we'd all still see each other, but she was right. It was never going to be like it was. All the fun and adventures we'd had.

Like when we skied on Mars. Or when we rode the roller coaster on the rings of Saturn. Or when my Aunts rescued me from a volcano.

I started to choke. "Or when you took me in and raised me like I was your own daughter," I said, and burst out crying.

"Now it's the happiest day of my life," said Aunt Hilda, as we all hugged and sobbed together.

Hey, I cry at weddings, all right??

Half an hour later, she and Will stood in front of the minister as he said, "I now pronounce you husband and wife." Aunt Hilda was married! Everybody cheered.

In the rush to grab the bouquet, Aunt Zelda knocked me over and broke my heel – but she did catch it.

"I'm getting married next," she cheered. "Everybody start shopping. I need flatwear and a bagel slicer."

"And a husband wouldn't hurt," I reminded her, before hobbling into the kitchen to fix my heel.

I found the deliveryman there, setting up the wedding cake. He was…gorgeous. We had one of those special moments when our eyes met. Like in a fairy tale when Prince Charming shows up.

On cue, he knelt down to fix my heel. "Who are you?" I asked. And why do I feel the urge to break my other heel?"

My heart was beating so fast I thought it was going to burst.

"My name's Luke," he told me. "And feel free to break it."

Just then, Harvey entered.

"Sabrina, I'm still in love with you," he said.

"But I know it'll never be returned, so I'm moving to California."

What?

Then Josh came in too.

"Sabrina, I can't ever see you again. I'm taking that newspaper job in Prague."

Huh??

"Well, it was nice meeting you," said Luke. "I guess I'll never see you again."

"Goodbye, Sabrina," they all said, before disappearing out of my life forever.

"Goodbye?" I gasped.

Then I remembered the deal I'd made with that Ed guy. This was it. I'd just sacrificed my true love.

But who was it? Harvey? Josh? Or Luke?

One of them was my soulmate, because when a witch loses her soulmate…

Yup. I froze. And fell to pieces.

Crazy ending, huh? Don't worry. Everything will be back to normal next time we meet. At least I hope so!

Love

Sabrina